R. Holmes & Co.

Other titles available from
Otto Penzler's Sherlock Holmes Library:

R. Holmes & Co.

Being the Remarkable Adventures
of Raffles Holmes, Esq.,
Detective and Amateur Cracksman
by Birth

BY

John Kendrick Bangs

ILLUSTRATED BY
Sydney Adamson

OTTO
PENZLER
BOOKS

NEW YORK

Copyright 1906 by Harper & Brothers
First published in 1906 by Harper & Brothers

Otto Penzler Books   Macmillan Publishing Company
129 West 56th Street   866 Third Avenue
New York, NY 10019   New York, NY 10022
(Editorial Offices only)

Maxwell Macmillan Canada, Inc.
1200 Eglinton Avenue East, Suite 200
Don Mills, Ontario M3C 3N1

Macmillan Publishing Company is part of the Maxwell Communication Group of Companies.

Library of Congress Cataloging-in-Publication Data
Bangs, John Kendrick, 1862–1922.
    R. Holmes & Co.: being the remarkable adventures of Raffles
  Holmes, Esq., detective and amateur cracksman by birth / by John
  Kendrick Bangs; illustrated by Sydney Adamson.
      p.   cm.
    ISBN 1-883402-63-8
    1. Private investigators—England—Fiction.   2. Criminals—
  England—Fiction.   I. Title.   II. Title: R. Holmes and
  Company.   III. Title: Raffles Holmes and Company.
  PS1064.B3R2   1994   813'.4—dc20   93-38798   CIP

10   9   8   7   6   5   4   3   2   1

Printed in the United States of America

With Apologies to

Sir Arthur Conan Doyle

and

Mr. E. W. Hornung

Contents

Illustrations

R. Holmes & Co.

"HE SILENTLY LANDED WITHIN REACH OF MY
HAND . . . AND PEERED IN THROUGH THE
OPEN WINDOW"

R. Holmes & Co.

I

INTRODUCING MR. RAFFLES HOLMES

IT was a blistering night in August. All day long the mercury in the thermometer had been flirting with the figures at the top of the tube, and the promised shower at night which a mendacious Weather Bureau had been prophesying as a slight mitigation of our sufferings was conspicuous wholly by its absence. I had but one comfort in the sweltering hours of the day, afternoon and evening, and that was that my family were away in the mountains, and there was no law against my sitting around all day clad only in my pajamas, and otherwise concealed from possibly intruding eyes by the wreaths of smoke that I extracted from the nineteen or twenty cigars which, when there is no protesting eye to suggest otherwise, form my daily allowance. I had tried every method known to the resourceful flat-dweller of modern times to get cool and to stay so, but, alas! it was impossible. Even the radiators, which all winter long had never once given forth a spark of heat, now hissed to the touch of my moistened finger. Enough cooling drinks to float an ocean greyhound had passed into my inner man, with no other result than to make me perspire more profusely than ever, and in so far as sensations went, to make me feel hotter than before. Finally, as a last resource, along about midnight, its gridiron floor having had a chance to lose some of its stored-up warmth,

Mr. Raffles Holmes

I climbed out upon the fire-escape at the rear of the Richmere, hitched my hammock from one of the railings thereof to the leader running from the roof to the area, and swung myself therein some eighty feet above the concreted pavement of our backyard—so called, perhaps, because of its dimensions which were just about that square. It was a little improvement, though nothing to brag of. What fitful zephyrs there might be, caused no doubt by the rapid passage to and fro on the roof above and fence-tops below of vagrom felines on Cupid's contentious battles bent, to the disturbance of the still air, soughed softly through the meshes of my hammock and gave some measure of relief, grateful enough for which I ceased the perfervid language I had been using practically since sunrise, and dozed off. And then there entered upon the scene that marvellous man,

R. Holmes & Co.

Raffles Holmes, of whose exploits it is the purpose of these papers to tell.

I had dozed perhaps for a full hour when the first strange sounds grated upon my ear. Somebody had opened a window in the kitchen of the first-floor apartment below, and with a dark lantern was inspecting the iron platform of the fire-escape without. A moment later this somebody crawled out of the window, and with movements that in themselves were a sufficient indication of the questionable character of his proceedings, made for the ladder leading to the floor above, upon which many a time and oft had I too climbed to home and safety when an inconsiderate janitor had locked me out. Every step that he took was stealthy—that much I could see by the dim starlight. His lantern he had turned dark again, evidently lest he should attract attention in the apartments

4

below as he passed their windows in his upward flight.

"Ha! ha!" thought I to myself. "It's never too hot for Mr. Sneak to get in his fine work. I wonder whose stuff he is after?"

Turning over flat on my stomach so that I might the more readily observe the man's movements, and breathing pianissimo lest he in turn should observe mine, I watched him as he climbed. Up he came as silently as the midnight mouse upon a soft carpet—up past the Jorkins apartments on the second floor; up stealthily by the Tinkletons' abode on the third; up past the fire-escape Italian garden of little Mrs. Persimmon on the fourth; up past the windows of the disagreeable Garraways' kitchen below mine, and then, with the easy grace of a feline, zip! he silently landed within reach of my hand on my own little iron veranda, and craning his neck to one side peered in through the open window and listened intently for two full minutes.

"Humph!" whispered my inner consciousness to itself. "He is the coolest thing I've seen since last Christmas left town. I wonder what he is up to? There's nothing in my apartment worth stealing, now that my wife and children are away, unless it be my Jap valet, Nogi, who might make a very excellent cab-driver if I could only find words to convey to his mind the idea that he is discharged."

And then the visitor, apparently having correctly assured himself that there was no one within, stepped across the window-sill and vanished into the darkness of my kitchen. A moment later I too entered the window in pursuit, not so close a one, however, as to acquaint him with my proximity. I wanted to see what the chap was up to; and also being totally unarmed and ignorant as to whether or not he carried dangerous weapons, I determined to go slow for a little while. Moreover, the situation was not wholly devoid of novelty, and it seemed to me that here at last was abundant opportunity for a new sensation. As he had entered, so did he walk cautiously along the narrow bowling-alley that serves for a hall-way connecting my drawing - room and library with the dining - room, until he came to the library, into which he disappeared. This was not reassuring to me, because, to tell the truth, I value my books more than I do my plate, and if I were to be robbed I should much have preferred his taking my plated plate from the dining - room than any one of my editions-de-luxe sets of the works of Marie Corelli, Hall Caine, and other standard authors from the library shelves. Once in the library he quietly drew the shades at the win-

dows thereof to bar possible intruding eyes from without, turned on the
electric lights, and proceeded to go
through my papers as calmly and
coolly as though they were his own.
In a short time, apparently, he found
what he wanted in the shape of a
royalty statement recently received
by me from my publishers, and,
lighting one of my cigars from a
bundle of brevas in front of him,
took off his coat and sat down to
peruse the statement of my returns.
Simple though it was, this act aroused
the first feeling of resentment in my
breast, for the relations between the
author and his publishers are among
the most sacred confidences of life,
and the peeping Tom who peers
through a key-hole at the courtship
of a young man engaged in wooing
his *fiancée* is no worse an intruder
than he who would tear aside the
veil of secrecy which screens the
official returns of a "best seller"

from the public eye. Feeling, therefore, that I had permitted matters to proceed as far as they might with propriety, I instantly entered the room and confronted my uninvited guest, bracing myself, of course, for the defensive onslaught which I naturally expected to sustain. But nothing of the sort occurred, for the intruder, with a composure that was nothing short of marvellous under the circumstances, instead of rising hurriedly like one caught in some disreputable act, merely leaned farther back in the chair, took the cigar from his mouth, and greeted me with:

"Howdy do, sir. What can I do for you this beastly hot night?"

The cold rim of a revolver-barrel placed at my temple could not more effectually have put me out of business than this nonchalant reception. Consequently I gasped out something about its being the sultriest 47th of August in eighteen years, and plumped back into a chair opposite him. "I wouldn't mind a Remsen cooler myself," he went on, "but the fact is your butler is off for to-night, and I'm hanged if I can find a lemon in the house. Maybe you'll join me in a smoke?" he added, shoving my own bundle of brevas across the table. "Help yourself."

"I guess I know where the lemons are," said I. "But how did you know my butler was out?"

"I telephoned him to go to Philadelphia this afternoon to see his brother Yoku, who is ill there," said my visitor. "You see, I didn't want him around to-night when I called. I knew I could manage you alone in case you turned up, as you see you have, but two of you, and one a Jap, I was afraid might involve us all in ugly complications. Between you and me, Jenkins, these Orientals are pretty lively fighters, and your man Nogi particularly has got jiu-jitsu down to a pretty fine point, so I had to do something to get rid of him. Our arrangement is a matter for two, not three, anyhow."

"So," said I, coldly. "You and I have an arrangement, have we? I wasn't aware of it."

"Not yet," he answered. "But there's a chance that we may have. If I can only satisfy myself that you are the man I'm looking for, there is no earthly reason that I can see why we should not come to terms. Go on out and get the lemons and the gin and soda, and let's talk this thing over man to man like a couple of good fellows at the club. I mean you no harm, and you certainly don't wish to do any kind of injury to a chap who, even though appearances are against him, really means to do you a good turn."

"Appearances certainly are against you, sir," said I, a trifle warmly, for the man's composure was irritating.

"A disappearance would be more likely to do you credit at this moment."

"Tush, Jenkins!" he answered. "Why waste breath saying self-evident things? Here you are on the verge of a big transaction, and you delay proceedings by making statements of fact, mixed in with a cheap wit which, I must confess, I find surprising, and so obvious as to be visible even to the blind. You don't talk like an author whose stuff is worth ten cents a word—more like a penny-a-liner, in fact, with whom words are of such small value that no one's the loser if he throws away a whole dictionary. Go out and mix a couple of your best Remsen coolers, and by the time you get back I'll have got to the gist of this royalty statement of yours, which is all I've come for. Your silver and books and love-letters and manuscripts are safe from me. I wouldn't have 'em as a gift."

Mr. Raffles Holmes

"What concern have you with my royalties?" I demanded.

"A vital one," said he. "Mix the coolers, and when you get back I'll tell you. Go on. There's a good chap. It 'll be daylight before long, and I want to close up this job if I can before sunrise."

What there was in the man's manner to persuade me to compliance with his wishes I am sure I cannot say definitely. There was a cold, steely glitter in his eye, for one thing, that, had I been a timid man, I might have found compelling on this special occasion, but it was this that bade me stay and fight him. With it, however, was a strengthfulness of purpose, a certain pleasant masterfulness, that, on the other hand, bade me feel that I could trust him, and it was to this aspect of his nature that I yielded. There was something frankly appealing in his long, thin, ascetic-looking face, and I found it irresistible.

R. Holmes & Co.

"All right," said I, with a smile and a frown to express the conflicting quality of my emotions. "So be it. I'll get the coolers, but you must remember, my friend, that there are coolers and coolers, just as there are jugs and jugs. The kind of jug that remains for you will depend upon the story you have to tell when I get back, so you'd better see that it's a good one."

"I am not afraid, Jenkins, old chap," he said, with a hearty laugh, as I rose up. "If this royalty statement can prove to me that you are the literary partner I need in my business, I can prove to you that I'm a good man to tie up to—so go along with you."

With this he lighted a fresh cigar and turned to a perusal of my statement, which, I am glad to say, was a good one, owing to the great success of my book, *Wild Animals I Have Never Met*—the seventh best seller at Rochester, Watertown, and Miami in June and July, 1905—while I went out into the dining-room and mixed the coolers. As you may imagine, I was not long at it, for my curiosity over my visitor lent wings to my corkscrew, and in five minutes I was back, with the tempting beverages in the tall glasses, the lemon curl giving it the vertebrate appearance that all stiff drinks should have, and the ice tinkling refreshingly upon the sultry air.

"There," said I, placing his glass before him. "Drink hearty, and then to business. Who are you?"

"There is my card," he replied, swallowing a goodly half of the cooler and smacking his lips appreciatively, and tossing a visiting-card across to me on the other side of the table. I picked up the card and read as follows: "Mr. Raffles Holmes, London and New York."

"Raffles Holmes?" I cried in amazement.

"The same, Mr. Jenkins," said he. "I am the son of Sherlock Holmes, the famous detective, and grandson of A. J. Raffles, the distinguished—er—ah—cricketer, sir."

I gazed at him, dumb with astonishment.

"You've heard of my father, Sherlock Holmes?" asked my visitor.

I confessed that the name of the gentleman was not unfamiliar to me.

"And Mr. Raffles, my grandfather?" he persisted.

"If there ever was a story of that fascinating man that I have not read, Mr. Holmes," said I, "I beg you will let me have it."

"Well, then," said he, with that quick, nervous manner which proved him a true son of Sherlock Holmes, "did it never occur to you as an extraordinary happening, as you read of my father's wonderful powers as a detective, and of Raffles's equally wonderful prowess as a—er—well, let us not mince words—as a thief, Mr. Jenkins, the two men operating in England at the same time, that no story ever appeared in which Sherlock Holmes's genius was pitted against the subtly planned misdeeds of Mr. Raffles? Is it not surprising that with two such men as they were, working out their destinies in almost identical grooves of daily action, they should never have crossed each other's paths as far as the public is the wiser, and in the very nature of the conflicting interests of their respective lines of action as foemen, the one pursuing, the other pursued, they should to the public's knowledge never have clashed?"

"Now that you speak of it," said I, "it was rather extraordinary that nothing of the sort happened. One would think that the sufferers from the depredations of Raffles would immediately have gone to Holmes for assistance in bringing the other to justice. Truly, as you intimate, it was strange that they never did."

"Pardon me, Jenkins," put in my visitor. "I never intimated anything of the sort. What I intimated was that no story of any such conflict ever came to light. As a matter of fact, Sherlock Holmes was put upon a Raffles case in 1883, and while success attended upon every step of it, and my grandfather was run to earth by him as easily as was ever any other criminal in Holmes's grip, a little naked god called Cupid stepped in, saved Raffles from jail, and wrote the word failure across Holmes's docket of the case. *I, sir, am the only tangible result of Lord Dorrington's retainers to Sherlock Holmes.*"

"You speak enigmatically, after the occasional fashion of your illustrious father," said I. "The Dorrington case is unfamiliar to me."

"Naturally so," said my *vis-à-vis*. "Because, save to my father, my grandfather, and myself, the details are unknown to anybody. Not even my mother knew of the incident, and as for Dr. Watson and Bunny, the scribes through whose industry the adventures of those two great men were respectively narrated to an absorbed world, they didn't even know there had ever been a Dorrington case, because Sherlock Holmes never told Watson and Raffles never told Bunny. But they both told me, and now that I am satisfied that there is a demand for your books, I am willing to tell it to you with the understanding that we share and share alike in the profits if perchance you think well enough of it to write it up."

"Go on!" I said. "I'll whack up with you square and honest."

"Which is more than either Watson or Bunny ever did with my father or my grandfather, else I should not be in the business which

now occupies my time and attention,"
said Raffles Holmes, with a cold snap
to his eyes which I took as an admo-
nition to hew strictly to the line of
honor, or to subject myself to terrible
consequences. "With that understanding, Jenkins, I'll tell you the
story of the Dorrington Ruby Seal,
in which some crime, a good deal of
romance, and my ancestry are involved."

II

THE ADVENTURE OF THE DORRING-
TON RUBY SEAL

"LORD DORRINGTON, as you
may have heard," said Raffles
Holmes, leaning back in my easy-chair
and gazing reflectively up at the ceiling, "was chiefly famous in England
as a sporting peer. His vast estates,
in five counties, were always open to
any sportsman of renown, or otherwise, as long as he was a true sportsman. So open, indeed, was the
house that he kept that, whether he
was there or not, little week-end
parties of members of the sporting
fraternity used to be got up at a
moment's notice to run down to Dorrington Castle, Devonshire; to Dor-

rington Lodge on the Isle of Wight;
to Dorrington Hall, near Dublin, or
to any other country place for over
Sunday.

"Sometimes there'd be a lot of
turf people; sometimes a dozen or
more devotees of the prize-ring; not
infrequently a gathering of the best-
known cricketers of the time, among
whom, of course, my grandfather, A.
J. Raffles, was conspicuous. For the
most part, the cricketers never par-
took of Dorrington's hospitality save
when his lordship was present, for
your cricket-player is a bit more
punctilious in such matters than your
turfmen or ring-side habitués. It so
happened one year, however, that his
lordship was absent from England
for the better part of eight months,
and, when the time came for the
annual cricket gathering at his Devonshire place, he cabled his London
representative to see to it that everything was carried on just as if he

The Dorrington Ruby Seal

were present, and that every one should be invited for the usual week's play and pleasure at Dorrington Castle. His instructions were carried out to the letter, and, save for the fact that the genial host was absent, the house-party went through to perfection. My grandfather, as usual, was the life of the occasion, and all went merry as a marriage-bell. Seven months later, Lord Dorrington returned, and, a week after that, the loss of the Dorrington jewels from the Devonshire strong-boxes was a matter of common knowledge. When, or by whom, they had been taken was an absolute mystery. As far as anybody could find out, they might have been taken the night before his return, or the night after his departure. The only fact in sight was that they were gone—Lady Dorrington's diamonds, a half-dozen valuable jewelled rings belonging to his lordship, and, most irremediable of losses, the

famous ruby seal which George IV.
had given to Dorrington's grandfather, Sir Arthur Deering, as a token
of his personal esteem during the
period of the Regency. This was a
flawless ruby, valued at some six
or seven thousand pounds sterling,
in which had been cut the Deering
arms surrounded by a garter upon
which were engraved the words,
'Deering Ton,' which the family,
upon Sir Arthur's elevation to the
peerage in 1836, took as its title, or
Dorrington. His lordship was almost prostrated by the loss. The
diamonds and the rings, although
valued at thirty thousand pounds,
he could easily replace, but the personal associations of the seal were
such that nothing, no amount of
money, could duplicate the lost
ruby."

"So that his first act," I broke in,
breathlessly, "was to send for—"

"Sherlock Holmes, my father,"

The Dorrington Ruby Seal

said Raffles Holmes. "Yes, Mr. Jenkins, the first thing Lord Dorrington did was to telegraph to London for Sherlock Holmes, requesting him to come immediately to Dorrington Castle and assume charge of the case. Needless to say, Mr. Holmes dropped everything else and came. He inspected the gardens, measured the road from the railway station to the castle, questioned all the servants; was particularly insistent upon knowing where the parlor-maid was on the 13th of January; secured accurate information as to the personal habits of his lordship's dachshund Nicholas; subjected the chef to a cross-examination that covered every point of his life, from his remote ancestry to his receipt for baking apples; gathered up three suit-cases of sweepings from his lordship's private apartment, and two boxes containing three each of every variety of cigars that Lord Dorrington had laid down in his cellar. As you are aware, Sherlock Holmes, in his prime, was a great master of detail. He then departed for London, taking with him an impression in wax of the missing seal, which Lord Dorrington happened to have preserved in his escritoire.

"On his return to London, Holmes inspected the seal carefully under a magnifying-glass, and was instantly impressed with the fact that it was not unfamiliar to him. He had seen it somewhere before, but where? That was now the question uppermost in his mind. Prior to this, he had never had any communication with Lord Dorrington, so that, if it was in his correspondence that the seal had formerly come to him, most assuredly the person who had used it had come by it dishonestly. Fortunately, at that time, it was a habit of my father's never to destroy papers of any sort. Every letter that he ever received was classified and filed, envelope and all. The thing to do, then, was manifestly to run over the files and find the letter, if indeed it was in or on a letter that the seal had first come to his attention. It was a herculean job, but that never feazed Sherlock Holmes, and he went at it tooth and nail. Finally his effort was rewarded. Under 'Applications for Autograph' he found a daintily scented little missive from a young girl living at Goring-Streatley on the Thames, the daughter, she said, of a retired missionary — the Reverend James Tattersby—asking him if he would not kindly write his autograph upon the enclosed slip for her collection. It was the regular stock application that truly distinguished men receive in every mail. The only thing to distinguish it from other applications was the beauty of the seal on the fly of the envelope, which attracted his passing notice and was then filed away with the other letters of similar import.

"'Ho! ho!' quoth Holmes, as he compared the two impressions and discovered that they were identical. 'An innocent little maiden who collects autographs, and a retired missionary in possession of the Dorrington seal, eh? Well, that *is* interesting. I think I shall run down to Goring-Streatley over Sunday and meet Miss Marjorie Tattersby and her reverend father. I'd like to see to what style of people I have intrusted my autograph.'

"To decide was to act with Sherlock Holmes, and the following Saturday, hiring a canoe at Windsor, he made his way up the river until he came to the pretty little hamlet, snuggling in the Thames Valley, if such it may be called, where the young lady and her good father were dwelling. Fortune favored him in that his prey was still there

The Dorrington Ruby Seal

—both much respected by the whole community; the father a fine looking, really splendid specimen of a man whose presence alone carried a conviction of integrity and lofty mind; the daughter—well, to see her was to love her, and the moment the eyes of Sherlock fell upon her face that great heart of his, that had ever been adamant to beauty, a very Gibraltar against the wiles of the other sex, went down in the chaos of a first and overwhelming passion. So hard hit was he by Miss Tattersby's beauty that his chief thought now was to avert rather than to direct suspicion towards her. After all, she might have come into possession of the jewel honestly, though how the daughter of a retired missionary, considering its intrinsic value, could manage such a thing, was pretty hard to understand, and he fled back to London to think it over. Arrived there, he found an invitation to visit

R. Holmes & Co.

Dorrington Castle again *incog*. Lord Dorrington was to have a mixed week-end party over the following Sunday, and this, he thought, would give Holmes an opportunity to observe the characteristics of Dorrington's visitors and possibly gain therefrom some clew as to the light-fingered person from whose depredations his lordship had suffered. The idea commended itself to Holmes, and in the disguise of a young American clergyman, whom Dorrington had met in the States, the following Friday found him at Dorrington Castle.

"Well, to make a long story short," said Raffles Holmes, "the young clergyman was introduced to many of the leading sportsmen of the hour, and, for the most part, they passed muster, but one of them did not, and that was the well-known cricketer A. J. Raffles, for the moment Raffles entered the room, jovially greeting everybody about him, and was pre-

The Dorrington Ruby Seal

sented to Lord Dorrington's new
guest, Sherlock Holmes recognized in
him no less a person than the Reverend James Tattersby, retired missionary of Goring-Streatley-on-Thames,
and the father of the woman who had
filled his soul with love and yearning
of the truest sort. The problem was
solved. Raffles was, to all intents
and purposes, caught with the goods
on. Holmes could have exposed him
then and there had he chosen to do
so, but every time it came to the
point the lovely face of Marjorie
Tattersby came between him and his
purpose. How could he inflict the
pain and shame which the exposure
of her father's misconduct would certainly entail upon that fair woman,
whose beauty and fresh innocence had
taken so strong a hold upon his heart?
No—that was out of the question.
The thing to do, clearly, was to visit
Miss Tattersby during her father's
absence, and, if possible, ascertain

from her just how she had come into
possession of the seal, before taking
further steps in the matter. This he
did. Making sure, to begin with, that
Raffles was to remain at Dorrington Hall for the coming ten days,
Holmes had himself telegraphed for
and returned to London. There he
wrote himself a letter of introduction
to the Reverend James Tattersby, on
the paper of the Anglo-American Missionary Society, a sheet of which he
secured in the public writing-room of
that institution, armed with which he
returned to the beautiful little spot
on the Thames where the Tatters-
bys abode. He spent the night at
the inn, and, in conversation with
the landlord and boatmen, learned
much that was interesting concerning
the Reverend James. Among other
things, he discovered that this gentleman and his daughter had been
respected residents of the place for
three years; that Tattersby was

rarely seen in the daytime about the place; that he was unusually fond of canoeing at night, which, he said, gave him the quiet and solitude necessary for that reflection which is so essential to the spiritual being of a minister of grace; that he frequently indulged in long absences, during which time it was supposed that he was engaged in the work of his calling. He appeared to be a man of some, but not of lavish, means. The most notable and suggestive thing, however, that Holmes ascertained in his conversation with the boatmen was that, at the time of the famous Cliveden robbery, when several thousand pounds' worth of plate had been taken from the great hall, that later fell into the possession of a well-known American hotel-keeper, Tattersby, who happened to be on the river late that night, was, according to his own statement, the unconscious witness of the escape of the thieves on board a mysterious steam-launch, which the police were never able afterwards to locate. They had nearly upset his canoe with the wash of their rapidly moving craft as they sped past him after having stowed their loot safely on board. Tattersby had supposed them to be employés of the estate, and never gave the matter another thought until three days later, when the news of the robbery was published to the world. He had immediately communicated the news of what he had seen to the police, and had done all that lay in his power to aid them in locating the robbers, but all to no purpose. From that day to this the mystery of the Cliveden plot had never been solved.

"The following day Holmes called at the Tattersby cottage, and was fortunate enough to find Miss Tattersby at home. His previous impression as to her marvellous beauty was more than confirmed, and each moment that he talked to her she revealed new graces of manner that completed the capture of his hitherto unsusceptible heart. Miss Tattersby regretted her father's absence. He had gone, she said, to attend a secret missionary conference at Pentwllycod in Wales, and was not expected back for a week, all of which quite suited Sherlock Holmes. Convinced that, after years of waiting, his affinity had at last crossed his path, he was in no hurry for the return of that parent, who would put an instant quietus upon this affair of the heart. Manifestly the thing for him to do was to win the daughter's hand, and then intercept the father, acquaint him with his aspirations, and compel acquiescence by the force of his knowledge of Raffles's misdeed. Hence, instead of taking his departure immediately, he remained at the Goring-Streatley Inn, taking care each day to encounter Miss Tattersby on one

pretext or another, hoping that their
acquaintance would ripen into friendship, and then into something warmer.
Nor was the hope a vain one, for when
the fair Marjorie learned that it was
the visitor's intention to remain in
the neighborhood until her father's
return, she herself bade him to make
use of the old gentleman's library, to
regard himself always as a welcome
daytime guest. She even suggested
pleasant walks through the neighbor-
ing country, little canoe trips up and
down the Thames, which they might
take together, of all of which Holmes
promptly availed himself, with the
result that, at the end of six days,
both realized that they were designed
for each other, and a passionate
declaration followed which opened
new vistas of happiness for both.
Hence it was that, when the Reverend
James Tattersby arrived at Goring-
Streatley the following Monday night,
unexpectedly, he was astounded to

find sitting together in the moonlight, in the charming little English garden at the rear of his dwelling, two persons, one of whom was his daughter Marjorie and the other a young American curate to whom he had already been introduced as A. J. Raffles.

"'We have met before, I think,' said Raffles, coldly, as his eye fell upon Holmes.

"'I—er—do not recall the fact,' replied Holmes, meeting the steely stare of the home-comer with one of his own flinty glances.

"'H'm!' ejaculated Raffles, nonplussed at the other's failure to recognize him. Then he shivered slightly. 'Suppose we go in-doors, it is a trifle chilly out here in the night air.'

"The whole thing, the greeting, the meeting, Holmes's demeanor and all, was so admirably handled that Marjorie Tattersby never guessed the truth, never even suspected the intense dramatic quality of the scene she had just gazed upon.

"'Yes, let us go in-doors,' she acquiesced. 'Mr. Dutton has something to say to you, papa.'

"'So I presumed,' said Raffles, dryly. 'And something that were better said to me alone, I fancy, eh?' he added.

"'Quite so,' said Holmes, calmly. And in-doors they went. Marjorie immediately retired to the drawing-room, and Holmes and Raffles went at once to Tattersby's study.

"'Well?' said Raffles, impatiently, when they were seated. 'I suppose you have come to get the Dorrington seal, Mr. Holmes.'

"'Ah—you know me, then, Mr. Raffles?' said Holmes, with a pleasant smile.

"'Perfectly,' said Raffles. 'I knew you at Dorrington Hall the moment I set eyes on you, and, if I hadn't, I should have known later, for the night

after your departure Lord Dorrington
took me into his confidence and revealed your identity to me.'

"'I am glad,' said Holmes. 'It
saves me a great deal of unnecessary
explanation. If you admit that you
have the seal—'

"'But I don't,' said Raffles. 'I
mentioned it a moment ago, because
Dorrington told me that was what
you were after. I haven't got it,
Mr. Holmes.'

"'I know that,' observed Holmes,
quietly. 'It is in the possession of
Miss Tattersby, your daughter, Mr.
Raffles.'

"'She showed it to you, eh?' demanded Raffles, paling.

"'No. She sealed a note to me
with it, however,' Holmes replied.

"'A note to you?' cried Raffles.

"'Yes. One asking for my autograph. I have it in my possession,'
said Holmes.

"'And how do you know that she

is the person from whom that note really came?' Raffles asked.

"'Because I have seen the autograph which was sent in response to that request in your daughter's collection, Mr. Raffles,' said Holmes.

"'So that you conclude—?' Raffles put in, hoarsely.

"'I do not conclude; I begin by surmising, sir, that the missing seal of Lord Dorrington was stolen by one of two persons—yourself or Miss Marjorie Tattersby,' said Holmes, calmly.

"'Sir!' roared Raffles, springing to his feet menacingly.

"'Sit down, please,' said Holmes. 'You did not let me finish. I was going to add, Dr. Tattersby, that a week's acquaintance with that lovely woman, a full knowledge of her peculiarly exalted character and guileless nature, makes the alternative of guilt that affects her integrity clearly preposterous, which, by a very simple process of elimination, fastens the guilt, beyond all peradventure, on your shoulders. At any rate, the presence of the seal in this house will involve you in difficult explanations. Why is it here? How did it come here? Why are you known as the Reverend James Tattersby, the missionary, at Goring-Streatley, and as Mr. A. J. Raffles, the cricketer and man of the world, at Dorrington Hall, to say nothing of the Cliveden plate—'

"'Damnation!' roared the Reverend James Tattersby again, springing to his feet and glancing instinctively at the long low book-shelves behind him.

"'To say nothing,' continued Holmes, calmly lighting a cigarette, 'of the Cliveden plate now lying concealed behind those dusty theological tomes of yours which you never allow to be touched by any other hand than your own.'

"'How did you know?' cried Raffles, hoarsely.

"'I didn't,' laughed Holmes. 'You have only this moment informed me of the fact!'

"There was a long pause, during which Raffles paced the floor like a caged tiger.

"'I'm a dangerous man to trifle with, Mr. Holmes,' he said, finally. 'I can shoot you down in cold blood in a second.'

"'Very likely,' said Holmes. 'But you won't. It would add to the difficulties in which the Reverend James Tattersby is already deeply immersed. Your troubles are sufficient, as matters stand, without your having to explain to the world why you have killed a defenceless guest in your own study in cold blood.'

"'Well—what do you propose to do?' demanded Raffles, after another pause.

"'Marry your daughter, Mr. Raf-

"'I'M A DANGEROUS MAN TO TRIFLE WITH, MR. HOLMES,' HE SAID"

fles, or Tattersby, whatever your permanent name is — I guess it's Tattersby in this case,' said Holmes. 'I love her and she loves me. Perhaps I should apologize for having wooed and won her without due notice to you, but you doubtless will forgive that. It's a little formality you sometimes overlook yourself when you happen to want something that belongs to somebody else.'

"What Raffles would have answered no one knows. He had no chance to reply, for at that moment Marjorie herself put her radiantly lovely little head in at the door with a 'May I come in?' and a moment later she was gathered in Holmes's arms, and the happy lovers received the Reverend James Tattersby's blessing. They were married a week later, and, as far as the world is concerned, the mystery of the Dorrington seal and that of the Cliveden plate was never solved.

"'It is compounding a felony, Raffles,' said Holmes, after the wedding, 'but for a wife like that, hanged if I wouldn't compound the ten commandments!'

"I hope," I ventured to put in at that point, "that the marriage ceremony was not performed by the Reverend James Tattersby."

"Not on your life!" retorted Raffles Holmes. "My father was too fond of my mother to permit of any flaw in his title. A year later I was born, and—well, here I am—son of one, grandson of the other, with hereditary traits from both strongly developed and ready for business. I want a literary partner — a man who will write me up as Bunny did Raffles, and Watson did Holmes, so that I may get a percentage on that part of the swag. I offer you the job, Jenkins. Those royalty statements show me that you are the man, and your books prove to me that you need a few fresh ideas.

The Dorrington Ruby Seal

Come, what do you say? Will you
do it?"

"My boy," said I, enthusiastically,
"don't say another word. Will I?
Well, just try me!"

And so it was that Raffles Holmes
and I struck a bargain and became
partners.

III

THE ADVENTURE OF MRS. BURLIN-GAME'S DIAMOND STOMACHER

I HAD seen the marvellous creation very often at the opera, and in many ways resented it. Not that I was in the least degree a victim to envy, hatred, and malice towards those who are possessed of a superabundance of this world's good things—far from it. I rejoice in the great fortunes of earth because, with every dollar corralled by the superior energies of the multi-millionaires, the fewer there are for other men to seek, and until we stop seeking dollars and turn our minds to other, finer things, there will be no hope of peace and sweet content upon this little green ball we inhabit. My resentment of Mrs. Burlingame's diamond stomacher was not then based on envy of its possession, but merely upon the twofold nuisance which it created at the opera-house, as the lady who wore it sat and listened to the strains of Wagner, Bizet, or Gounod, mixed in with the small-talk of Reggie Stockson, Tommie de Coupon, and other lights of the social firmament. In the first place, it caused the people sitting about me in the high seats of the opera-house to chatter about it and discuss its probable worth every time the lady made her appearance in it, and I had fled from the standee part of the house to the top gallery just to escape the talkers, and, if possible, to get my music straight, without interruptions of any sort whatsoever on the side. In the second place, the confounded thing glittered so that, from where I sat, it was as dazzling as so many small mirrors flashing in the light of the sun. It seemed as if every electric light in the house found some kind of a refractor in the thousands of gems of which it was composed, and many of the brilliant light effects of the stage were dimmed in their lustre by the persistent intrusion of Mrs. Burlingame's glory upon my line of vision.

Hence it was that, when I picked up my morning paper and read in great flaring head-lines on the front page that Mrs. Burlingame's diamond stomacher had been stolen from her at her Onyx Cottage at Newport, I smiled broadly, and slapped the breakfast-table so hard in my satisfaction that even the shredded-wheat biscuits flew up into the air and caught in the chandelier.

"Thank Heaven for that!" I said. "Next season I shall be able to enjoy my opera undisturbed."

I little thought, at that blissful moment, how closely indeed were my own fortunes to be connected with that wonderful specimen of the jeweller's handicraft, but an hour later I was made aware of the first link in the chain that, in a measure, bound me to it. Breakfast over, I went to my desk to put the finishing touches to a novel I had written the week before, when word came up on the telephone from below that a gentleman from *Busybody's Magazine* wished to see me on an important matter of business.

"Tell him I'm already a subscriber," I called down, supposing the visitor to be merely an agent. "I took the magazine, and a set of Chaucer in a revolving bookcase, from one of their agents last month and have paid my dollar."

In a moment another message came over the wire.

"The gentleman says he wants to see you about writing a couple of full-page sonnets for the Christmas number," the office man 'phoned up.

"Show him up," I replied, instantly.

Two minutes later a rather handsome man, with a fine eye and a long, flowing gray beard, was ushered into my apartment.

"I am Mr. Stikes, of *Busybody's*, Mr. Jenkins," he said, with a twinkle in his eye. "We thought you might like to contribute to our Christmas issue. We want two sonnets, one on the old Christmas and the other on the new. We can't offer you more than a thousand dollars apiece for them, but—"

Something caught in my throat, but I managed to reply. "I might shade my terms a trifle since you want as many as two," I gurgled. "And I assume you will pay on acceptance?"

"Certainly," he said, gravely. "Could you let me have them, say— this afternoon?"

I turned away so that he would not see the expression of joy on my

face, and then there came from behind me a deep chuckle and the
observation in a familiar voice:

"You might throw in a couple of
those Remsen coolers, too, while
you're about it, Jenkins."

I whirled about as if struck, and
there, in place of the gray-bearded
editor, stood—Raffles Holmes.

"Bully disguise, eh!" he said, fold-
ing up his beard and putting it in his
pocket.

"Ye-e-es," said I, ruefully, as I
thought of the vanished two thousand. "I think I preferred you in
disguise, though, old man," I added.

"You won't when you hear what
I've come for," said he. "There's
$5000 apiece in this job for us."

"To what job do you refer?" I asked.

"The Burlingame case," he replied.
"I suppose you read in the papers
this morning how Mrs. Burlingame's
diamond stomacher has turned up
missing."

"Yes," said I, "and I'm glad of it."

"You ought to be," said Holmes, "since it will put $5000 in your pocket. You haven't heard yet that there is a reward of $10,000 offered for its recovery. The public announcement has not yet been made, but it will be in to-night's papers, and we are the chaps that are going to get the reward."

"But how?" I demanded.

"Leave that to me," said he. "By-the-way, I wish you'd let me leave this suit-case of mine in your room for about ten days. It holds some important papers, and my shop is turned topsy-turvy just now with the painters."

"Very well," said I. "I'll shove it under my bed."

I took the suit-case as Holmes had requested, and hid it away in my bedroom, immediately returning to the library, where he sat smoking one of my cigars as cool as a cucumber. There was something in his eye, however, that aroused my suspicion as soon as I entered.

"See here, Holmes," said I. "I can't afford to be mixed up in any shady business like this, you know. Have you got that stomacher?"

"No, I haven't," said he. "Honor bright—I haven't."

I eyed him narrowly.

"I think I understand the evasion," I went on. "*You* haven't got it because I have got it—it's in that suit-case under my bed."

"Open it and see for yourself," said he. "It isn't there."

"But you know where it is?" I demanded.

"How else could I be sure of that $10,000 reward?" he asked.

"Where is it?" I demanded.

"It—er—it isn't located yet—that is, not finally," said he. "And it won't be for ten days. Ten days from now Mrs. Burlingame will find it herself and we'll divvy on the reward, my boy, and not a trace of dishonesty in the whole business."

And with that Raffles Holmes filled his pockets with cigars from my stores, and bidding me be patient went his way.

The effect of his visit upon my nerves was such that any more work that day was impossible. The fear of possible complications to follow upset me wholly, and, despite his assurance that the suit-case was innocent of surreptitiously acquired stomachers, I could not rid my mind of the suspicion that he made of my apartment a fence for the conceal-ment of his booty. The more I thought of it the more was I inclined to send for him and request him to remove the bag forthwith, and yet, if it should so happen that he had spoken the truth, I should by that act endanger our friendship and pos-sibly break the pact, which bade fair to be profitable. Suddenly I remembered his injunction to me to look for myself and see if the stomacher really was concealed there, and I hastened to act upon it. It might have been pure bluff on his part, and I resolved not to be bluffed.

The case opened easily, and the moment I glanced into it my suspicions were allayed. It contained nothing but bundle after bundle of letters tied together with pink and blue ribbons, one or two old daguerreotypes, some locks of hair, and an ivory miniature of Raffles Holmes himself as an infant. Not a stomacher, diamond or otherwise, was hid in the case, nor any other suspicious object, and I closed it with a sheepish feeling of shame for having intruded upon the sacred correspondence and relics of the happy childhood days of my new friend.

That night, as Holmes had asserted, a reward of $10,000 was offered for the recovery of the Burlingame stomacher, and the newspapers for the next ten days were full of the theories of detectives of all sorts, amateur, professional, and reportorial. Central Office was after it in one place, others sought it elsewhere. The editor of one New York paper printed a full list of the names of the guests at Mrs. Burlingame's dinner the night the treasure was stolen, and, whether they ever discovered it for themselves or not, several bearers of highly honored social names were shadowed by reporters and others everywhere they went for the next week. At the end of five days the reward was increased to $20,000, and then Raffles Holmes's name began to appear in connection with the case. Mrs. Burlingame herself had sent for him, and, without taking it out of the hands of others, had personally requested him to look into the matter. He had gone to Newport and looked the situation

The Diamond Stomacher

over there. He had questioned all
the servants in her two establish-
ments at Newport and New York,
and had finally assured the lady that,
on the following Tuesday morning,
he would advise her by wire of the
definite location of her missing jewel.

During all this time Holmes had
not communicated with me at all,
and I began to fear that, offended
by my behavior at our last meeting,
he had cut me out of his calculations
altogether, when, just as I was about
to retire on Sunday night, he reappeared as he had first come to me—
stealing up the fire-escape; and this
time he wore a mask, and carried un-
questionably a burglar's kit and a
dark lantern. He started nervously
as he caught sight of me reaching
up to turn off the light in the
library.

"Hang it all, Jenkins!" he cried.
"I thought you'd gone off to the
country for the week-end."

"No," said I. "I meant to go, but I was detained. What's up?"

"Oh, well—I may as well out with it," he answered. "I didn't want you to know, but—well, watch and see."

With this Raffles Holmes strode directly to my bookcase, removed my extra-illustrated set of Fox's *Book of Martyrs*, in five volumes, from the shelves, and there, resting upon the shelf behind them, glittered nothing less than the missing stomacher!

"Great Heavens, Holmes!" I said, "what does this mean? How did those diamonds get there?"

"I put them there myself while you were shoving my suit-case under your bed the other night," said he.

"You told me you didn't have them," I said, reproachfully.

"I didn't when I spoke—*you* had them," said he.

"You told me they had not been finally located," I persisted, angrily.

The Diamond Stomacher

"I told you the truth. They were only temporarily located," he answered. "I'm going to locate them definitely to-night, and to-morrow Mrs. Burlingame will find them—"

"Where?" I cried.

"*In her own safe in her New York house!*" said Raffles Holmes.

"You—"

"Yes—I took them from Newport myself — very easy job, too," said Raffles Holmes. "Ever since I saw them at the opera last winter I have had this in mind, so when Mrs. Burlingame gave her dinner I served as an extra butler from Delmonico's— drugged the regular chap on the train on his way up from New York—took his clothes, and went in his place. That night I rifled the Newport safe of the stomacher, and the next day brought it here. To-night I take it to the Burlingame house on Fifth Avenue, secure entrance through a basement door, to which, in my capacity of detective, I have obtained the key, and, while the caretakers sleep, Mrs. Burlingame's diamond stomacher will be placed in the safe on the first floor back.

"To-morrow morning I shall send Mrs. Burlingame this message: '*Have you looked in your New York safe?* [Signed] Raffles Holmes,'" he continued. "She will come to town by the first train to find out what I mean; we will go to her residence; she will open the safe, and—$20,000 for us."

"By Jove! Holmes, you are a wonder," said I. "This stomacher is worth $250,000 at the least," I added, as I took the creation in my hand. "Pot of money that!"

"Yes," said he, with a sigh, taking the stomacher from me and fondling it. "The Raffles in me tells me that, but the Sherlock Holmes in my veins —well, I can't keep it, Jenkins, if that is what you mean."

I blushed at the intimation con-

"'THAT NIGHT I RIFLED THE NEWPORT SAFE OF
THE STOMACHER'"

veyed by his words, and was silent; and Holmes, gathering up his tools and stuffing the stomacher in the capacious bosom of his coat, bade me *au revoir*, and went out into the night.

The rest is already public property. All the morning papers were full of the strange recovery of the Burlingame stomacher the following Tuesday morning, and the name of Raffles Holmes was in every mouth. That night, the very essence of promptitude, Holmes appeared at my apartment and handed me a check for my share in the transaction.

"Why—what does this mean?" I cried, as I took in the figures; "$12,-500—I thought it was to be only $10,000."

"It was," said Raffles Holmes, "but Mrs. Burlingame was so overjoyed at getting the thing back she made the check for $25,000 instead of for $20,000."

"You're the soul of honor, Holmes!" I murmured.

"On my father's side," he said, with a sigh. "On my mother's side it comes hard."

"And Mrs. Burlingame—didn't she ask you how you ferreted the thing out?" I asked.

"Yes," said Holmes. "But I told her that that was my secret, that my secret was my profession, and that my profession was my bread and butter."

"But she must have asked you who was the guilty person?" I persisted.

"Yes," said Holmes, "she did, and I took her for a little gallop through the social register, in search of the guilty party; that got on her nerves, so that when it came down to an absolute question of identity she begged me to forget it."

"I am dull of comprehension, Raffles," said I. "Tell me exactly what you mean."

The Diamond Stomacher

"Simply this," said Raffles Holmes. "The present four hundred consists of about 19,250 people, of whom about twenty-five per cent. go to Newport at one time or another—say, 4812. Of these 4812 about ten per cent. are eligible for invitations to the Burlingame dinners, or 480. Now whom of the 480 possibilities having access to the Burlingame cottage would we naturally suspect? Surely only those who were in the vicinity the night of the robbery. By a process of elimination we narrowed them down to just ten persons exclusive of Mrs. Burlingame herself and her husband, old Billie Burlingame. We took the lot and canvassed them. There were Mr. and Mrs. Willington Bodfish— they left early and the stomacher was known to be safe at the time of their departure. There were Bishop and Mrs. Pounderby, neither of whom would be at all likely to come back in the dead of the night and remove property that did not belong to them. There were Senator and Mrs. Jorrocks. The Senator is after bigger game than diamond stomachers, and Mrs. Jorrocks is known to be honest. There were Harry Gaddsby and his wife. Harry doesn't know enough to go in when it rains, and is too timid to call even his soul his own, so he couldn't have taken it; and Mrs. Gaddsby is long on stomachers, having at least five, and therefore would not be likely to try to land a sixth by questionable means. In that way we practically cleared eight possibilities of suspicion.

"'Now, Mrs. Burlingame,' said I, 'that leaves four persons still in the ring — yourself, your husband, your daughter, and the Duke of Snarleyow, your daughter's newly acquired *fiancé*, in whose honor the dinner was given. Of these four, you are naturally yourself the first to be acquitted. Your husband comes next, and is not likely to be the guilty party, because if he wants a diamond stomacher he needn't steal it, having money enough to buy a dozen of them if he wishes. The third, your daughter, should be regarded as equally innocent, because if she was really desirous of possessing the jewel all she had to do was to borrow it from you. That brings us down to the Duke of—'

"'Hush! I beg of you, Mr. Raffles Holmes!' she cried, in great agitation. 'Not another word, I beseech you! If any one should overhear us— The subject, after all, is an unprofitable one, and I'd—I'd rather drop it, and it—it—er—it has just occurred to me that possibly I—er—possibly I—'

"'Put the jewel in the safe yourself?' I suggested.

"'Yes,' said Mrs. Burlingame, with a grateful glance and a tremendous sigh of relief. 'Now that I think of it, Mr. Raffles Holmes—that *was* it. I—er—I remember perfectly that—

er—that I didn't wear it at all the night of my little dinner, and that I *did* leave it behind me when I left town.'"

"Humph!" said I. "That may account for the extra $5000—"

"It may," said Raffles Holmes, pursing his lips into a deprecatory smile.

IV

THE ADVENTURE OF THE MISSING PENDANTS

"I THINK," said Raffles Holmes, as he ran over his expense account while sitting in my library one night some months ago, "that in view of the present condition of my exchequer, my dear Jenkins, it behooveth me to get busy. Owning a motor-car is a demned expensive piece of business, and my balance at the bank has shrunk to about $1683.59, thanks to my bills for cogs, clutches, and gasoline, plus the chauffeur's fines."

"In what capacity shall you work, Raffles or Holmes?" I asked, pausing in my writing and regarding him with that affectionate interest which contact with him had inspired in me.

"Play the combination always, Jenkins," he replied. "If I did the Raffles act alone, I should become a billionaire in this land of silk and money, your rich are so careless of their wealth — but where would my conscience be? On the other hand, if I stuck to the Holmes act exclusively, I'd starve to death; but the combination—ah—there is moderate fortune, my boy, with peace of mind thrown in."

Here he rose up, buttoned his coat about his spare figure, and reached out for his hat.

"I guess I'll tackle that case of the missing pendants to-morrow," he continued, flicking the ash from his cigar and gazing up at the ceiling with that strange twist in his eye which I had learned to regard as the harbinger of a dawning idea in his mind. "There's ten thousand dollars for somebody in that job, and you and I might as well have it as any one else."

"I'm ready," said I, as well I might be, for all I had to do in the matter was to record the adventure and take my half of the profits—no very difficult proceeding in either case.

"Good," quoth he. "I'll go to Gaffany & Co. to-morrow and offer my services."

"You have a clew?" I asked.

"I have an idea," he answered. "As for the lost diamonds, I know no more of their whereabouts than you do, but I shall be able beyond all question to restore to Gaffany & Co. two pendants just as good as those they have lost, and if I do that I am entitled to the reward, I fancy, am I not?"

"Most certainly," said I. "But where the dickens will you find two such stones? They are worth

$50,000 apiece, and they must match perfectly the two remaining jewels which Gaffany & Co. have· in their safe."

"I'll match 'em so closely that their own mother couldn't tell 'em apart," said Holmes, with a chuckle.

"Then the report that they are of such rarity of cut and lustre is untrue?" I asked.

"It's perfectly true," said Holmes, "but that makes no difference. The two stones that I shall return two weeks from to-day to Gaffany & Co. will be as like the two they have as they are themselves. Ta-ta, Jenkins —you can count on your half of that ten thousand as surely as though it jingled now in your pockets."

And with that Raffles Holmes left me to my own devices.

I presume that most readers of the daily newspapers are tolerably familiar with the case of the missing pendants to which Holmes referred,

The Missing Pendants

and on the quest for which he was now about to embark. There may be some of you, however, who have never heard of the mysterious robbery of Gaffany & Co., by which two diamonds of almost matchless purity—half of a quartet of these stones—pear-shaped and valued at $50,000 each, had disappeared almost as if the earth had opened and swallowed them up. They were a part of the famous Gloria Diamond, found last year at Kimberley, a huge, uncut gem of such value that no single purchaser for it could be found in the world. By a syndicate arrangement Gaffany & Co. had assumed charge of it, and were in the process of making for a customer a bar with four pendants cut from the original, when two of them disappeared. They had been last seen in the hands of a trusted employé of many years' standing, to whom they had been intrusted for mounting, and he had

been seen to replace them, at the end
of the day's work, in the little cage-
like office of the custodian of the safe
in which jewels of great value were
kept at night. This was the last seen
of them, and although five weeks had
elapsed since the discovery of their
loss and Holmes's decision to look
into the matter, no clew of the slightest description had been discovered
by the thousands of sleuths, professional or amateur, who had interested themselves in the case.

"He has such assurance!" I muttered. "To hear him talk one would
almost believe that they were already
in his possession."

I did not see Raffles Holmes again
for five days, and then I met him only
by chance, nor should I have known
it was he had he not made himself
known to me. I was on my way up-
town, a little after six o'clock, and
as I passed Gaffany's an aged man
emerged from the employés' en-

The Missing Pendants

trance, carrying a small bag in his hand. He was apparently very near-sighted, for he most unceremoniously bumped into me as he came out of the door on to the sidewalk.

Deference to age has always been a weakness of mine, and I apologized, although it was he that was at fault.

"Don't mention it, Jenkins," he whispered. "You are just the man I want to see. Café Panhard—to-night—eleven o'clock. Just happen in, and if a foreign-looking person with a red beard speaks to you don't throw him down, but act as if you were not annoyed by his mistake."

"You know me?" I asked.

"Tush, man—I'm Raffles Holmes!" and with that he was off.

His make-up was perfect, and as he hobbled his way along Broadway through the maze of cars, trucks, and hansoms, there was not in any part of him a hint or a suggestion that brought to mind my alert partner.

R. Holmes & Co.

Of course my excitement was intense. I could hardly wait for eleven o'clock to come, and at 9.30 I found myself in front of the Café Panhard a full hour and a half ahead of time, and never were there more minutes in that period of waiting than there seemed to be then as I paced Broadway until the appointed hour. It seemed ages before the clock down in front of the Whirald Building pointed to 10.55, but at last the moment arrived, and I entered the café, taking one of the little tables in the farther corner, where the light was not unduly strong and where the turmoil of the Hungarian band was reduced by distance from moltofortissimo to a moderate approach to a pianissimo, which would admit of conversation. Again I had to wait, but not for so long a time. It was twenty minutes past eleven when a fine-looking man of military bearing, wearing a full red beard,

The Missing Pendants

entered, and after looking the café over, sauntered up to where I sat.

"Good-evening, Mr. Jenkins," said he, with a slight foreign accent. "Are you alone?"

"Yes," said I.

"If you don't mind, I should like to sit here for a few moments," he observed, pulling out the chair opposite me. "I have your permission?"

"Certainly, Mr.—er—"

"Robinstein is my name," said he, sitting down, and producing a letter from his pocket. "I have here a note from my old friend Raffles Holmes—a note of introduction to you. I am a manufacturer of paste jewels—or rather was. I have had one or two misfortunes in my business, and find myself here in America practically stranded."

"Your place of business was—"

"In the Rue de l'Echelle in Paris," he explained. "I lost everything in unfortunate speculation, and have come here to see if I could not get a new start. Mr. Holmes thinks you can use your influence with Markoo & Co., the theatrical costumers, who, I believe, manufacture themselves all the stage jewelry they use in their business, to give me something to do. It was said in Paris that the gems which I made were of such quality that they would deceive, for a time, anyhow, the most expert lapidaries, and if I can only get an opening with Markoo & Co. I am quite confident that you will not repent having exerted your good offices in my behalf."

"Why, certainly, Mr. Robinstein," said I. "Any friend of Raffles Holmes may command my services. I know Tommy Markoo very well, and as this is a pretty busy time with him, getting his stuff out for the fall productions, I have little doubt I shall be able to help you. By Jove!" I added, as I glanced over the café, "that's a singular coincidence—there is Markoo himself just coming in the doorway."

"Really?" said Mr. Robinstein, turning and gazing towards the door. "He's a different-looking chap from what I had imagined. Perhaps, Mr. Jenkins, it would—er—expedite matters if you—"

"Of course," I interrupted. "Tommy is alone—we'll have him over."

And I beckoned to Markoo and invited him to join us.

"Good!" said he, in his whole-souled way. "Glad to have a chance to see you—I'm so confoundedly busy these days—just think of it, I've been at the shop ever since eight o'clock this morning."

"Tommy, I want to introduce you to my friend Mr. Robinstein," said I.

"Not Isidore Robinstein, of Paris?" said Markoo.

"I have that misfortune, Mr. Markoo," said Robinstein.

"Misfortune? Gad, Mr. Robinstein, we look at things through different glasses," returned Markoo. "The man who can do your work ought never to suffer misfortune—"

"If he only stays out of the stockmarket," said Robinstein.

"Aha," laughed Tommy. "Et tu, Brute?"

We all aughed, and if there was any ice to be broken after that it was along the line of business of the café. We got along famously together, and when we parted company, two hours later, all the necessary arrangements had been made for Mr. Robinstein to begin at once with Markoo—the following day, in fact.

Four nights later Holmes turned up at my apartment.

"Well," said I, "have you come to report progress?"

"Yes," he said. "The reward will arrive on time, but it's been the de'il's own job. Pretty, aren't they!" he added, taking a small package wrapped in tissue-paper out of his pocket, and disclosing its contents.

"Gee-rusalem, what beauties!" I cried, as my eyes fell on two such diamonds as I had never before seen. They sparkled on the paper like bits of sunshine, and that their value was quite $100,000 it did not take one like myself, who knew little of gems, to see at a glance. "You have found them, have you?"

"Found what?" asked Raffles Holmes.

"The missing pendants," said I.

"Well—not exactly," said Raffles Holmes. "I think I'm on the track of them, though. There's an old chap who works beside me down at Gaffany's who spends so much of his time drinking ice-water that I'm getting to be suspicious of him."

I roared with laughter.

"The ice-water habit is evidence of a criminal nature, eh?" I queried.

"Not per se," said Holmes, gravely, "but in conjunctibus—if my Latin is weak, please correct me—it is a very suspicious habit. When I see a man drink ten glasses of water in two hours it indicates to my mind that there is something in the water-cooler that takes his mind off his business. It is not likely to be either the ice or the water, on the doctrine of probabilities. Hence it must be something else. I caught him yesterday with his hand in it."

"His hand? In the water-cooler?" I demanded.

"Yes," said Holmes. "He said he was fishing around for a little piece of ice to cool his head, which ached, but I think differently. He got as pale as a ghost when I started in to fish for a piece for myself because my head ached too. I think he took the diamonds and has hid them there, but I'm not sure yet, and in my business I can't afford to make mistakes. If my suspicions are correct, he is merely awaiting his opportunity to fish them out and light out with them."

"Then these," I said, "are—are they paste?"

"No, indeed, they're the real thing," said Raffles Holmes, holding up one of the gems to the light, where it fairly coruscated with brilliance "These are the other two of the original quartet."

"Great Heavens, Holmes—do you mean to say that Gaffany & Co. permit you to go about with things like this in your pocket?" I demanded.

"Not they," laughed Holmes. "They'd have a fit if they knew I had 'em, only they don't know it."

"But how have you concealed the fact from them?" I persisted.

"Robinstein made me a pair exactly like them," said Holmes. "The paste ones are now lying in the Gaffany safe, where I saw them placed before leaving the shop to-night."

"You're too deep for me, Holmes," said I. "What's the game?"

"Now don't say game, Jenkins," he protested. "I never indulge in games. My quarry is not a game, but a scheme. For the past two weeks, with three days off, I have been acting as a workman in the Gaffany shop, wit the ostensible purpose of keeping my eye on ertain employés who are under suspicion. Each day the remaining two pendant-stones — these — have been handed to me to work on, merely to carry out the illusion. The first day, in odd moments, I made sketches of them, and on the night of the second I had 'em down in such detail as to cut and color, that Robinstein had no difficulty in reproducing them in the materials at his disposal in Markoo's shop. And to-night all I had to do to get them was to keep them and hand in the Robinstein substitutes when the hour of closing came."

"So that now, in place of four $50,000 diamonds, Gaffany & Co. are in possession of—"

"Two paste pendants, worth about $40 apiece," said Holmes. "If I fail to find the originals I shall have to use the paste ones to carry the scheme through, but I hate to do it. It's so confoundly inartistic and as old a trick as the pyramids."

"And to-morrow—"

Raffles Holmes got up and paced the floor nervously.

"Ah, Jenkins," he said, with a heart-rending sigh, "that is the point. To-morrow! Heavens! what will to-morrow's story be? I — I cannot tell."

"What's the matter, Holmes?" said I. "Are you in danger?"

"Physically, no—morally, my God! Jenkins, yes. I shall need all of your help," he cried.

"What can I do?" I asked. "You know you have only to command me,"

"Don't leave me this night for a minute," he groaned. "If you do, I am lost. The Raffles in me is rampant when I look at those jewels and think of what they will mean if I keep them. An independent fortune forever. All I have to do is to get aboard a ship and go to Japan and live in comfort the rest of my days with this wealth in my possession, and all the instincts of honesty that I possess, through the father in me, will be powerless to prevent my indulgence in this crime. Keep me in sight, and if I show the slightest inclination to give you the slip, knock me over the head will you, for my own good?"

I promised faithfully that I would do as he asked, but, as an easier way out of an unpleasant situation, I drugged his Remsen cooler with a

The Missing Pendants

sleeping-powder, and an hour later he was lying off on my divan lost to the world for eight hours at least. As a further precaution I put the jewels in my own safe.

The night's sleep had the desired effect, and with the returning day Holmes's better nature asserted itself. Raffles was subdued, and he returned to Gaffany's to put the finishing touches to his work.

"Here's your check, Jenkins," said Raffles Holmes, handing me a draft for $5000. "The gems were found to-day in the water-cooler in the workroom, and Gaffany & Co. paid up like gentlemen."

"And the thief?" I asked.

"Under arrest," said Raffles Holmes. "We caught him fishing for them."

"And your paste jewels, where are they?"

"I wish I knew," he answered, his face clouding over. "In the excite-

ment of the moment of the arrest I
got 'em mixed with the originals I
had last night, and they didn't give
me time or opportunity to pick 'em
out. The four were mounted immediately and sent under guard to
the purchåser. Gaffany & Co. didn't
want to keep them a minute longer
than was necessary. But the pur-
chaser is so rich he will never have
to sell 'em — so, you see, Jenkins,
we're as safe as a church."

"Your friend Robinstein was a
character, Holmes," said I.

"Yes," sighed Holmes. "Poor
chap—he was a great loss to his
friends. He taught me the art of
making paste gems when I was in
Paris. I miss him like the dickens."

"Miss him!" said I, getting anxious
for Robinstein. "What's happened?
He isn't—"

"Dead," said Holmes. "Two years
ago—dear old chap."

"Oh, come now, Holmes," I said.

"'WE CAUGHT HIM FISHING FOR THEM'"

The Missing Pendants

"What new game is this you are rigging on me? I met him only five nights ago—and you know it."

"Oh — that one," said Raffles Holmes, with a laugh. "*I* was that Robinstein."

"You?" I cried.

"Yes, me," said Holmes. "You don't suppose I'd let a third party into our secret, do you?"

And then he gave me one of those sweet, wistful smiles that made the wonder of the man all the greater.

"I wish to the dickens I knew whether these were real or paste!" he muttered, taking the extra pendants from his wallet as he spoke. "I don't dare ask anybody, and I haven't got any means of telling myself."

"Give them to me," said I, sternly, noting a glitter in his eye that suggested the domination for the moment of the Raffles in him.

"Tush, Jenkins," he began, uneasily.

87

"Give them to me, or I'll brain you, Holmes," said I, standing over him with a soda-water bottle gripped in my right hand, "for your own good. Come, give up."

He meekly obeyed.

"Come now, get on your hat," said I. "I want you to go out with me."

"What for, Jenkins?" he almost snarled.

"You'll see what for," said I.

And Raffles Holmes obeying, we walked down to the river's edge, where I stood for a moment, and then hurled the remaining stones far out into the waters.

Holmes gave a gasp and then a sigh of relief.

"There," I said. "It doesn't matter much to us now whether the confounded things were real or not."

V

THE ADVENTURE OF THE BRASS CHECK

"JENKINS," said Raffles Holmes to me the other night as we sat in my den looking over the criminal news in the evening papers, in search of some interesting material for him to work on, "this paper says that Mrs. Wilbraham Ward - Smythe has gone to Atlantic City for a week, and will lend her gracious presence to the social functions of the Hotel Garrymore, at that interesting city by the sea, until Monday, the 27th, when she will depart for Chicago, where her sister is to be married on the 29th. How would you like to spend the week with me at the Garrymore?"

"It all depends upon what we are

going for," said I. "Also, what in
thunder has Mrs. Wilbraham Ward-
Smythe got to do with us, or we with
her?"

"Nothing at all," said Holmes.
"That is, nothing much."

"Who is she?" I asked, eying him
suspiciously.

"All I know is what I have seen
in the papers," said Holmes. "She
came in on the *Altruria* two weeks
ago, and attracted considerable attention by declaring $130,000 worth
of pearl rope that she bought in Paris, instead of, woman-like, trying to
smuggle it through the custom-house.
It broke the heart of pretty nearly
every inspector in the service. She'd
been watched very carefully by the
detective bureau in Paris, and when
she purchased the rope there, the
news of it was cabled over in cipher,
so that they'd all be on the lookout
for it when she came in. The whole
force on the pier was on the qui vive,

and one of the most expert women searchers on the pay-roll was detailed to give her special attention the minute she set foot on shore; but instead of doing as they all believed she would do, and giving the inspectors a chance to catch her at trying to evade the duties, to their very great profit, she calmly and coolly declared the stuff, paid her little sixty-five per cent. like a major, and drove off to the Castoria in full possession of her jewels. The Collector of the Port had all he could do to keep 'em from draping the custom-house for thirty days, they were all so grief-stricken. She'll probably take the rope to Atlantic City with her."

"Aha!" said I. "That's the milk in the cocoanut, is it? You're after that pearl rope, are you, Raffles?"

"On my honor as a Holmes," said he, "I am not. I shall not touch the pearl rope, although I have no doubt that I shall have some unhappy moments during the week that I am in the same hotel with it. That's one reason why I'd like to have you go along, Jenkins—just to keep me out of temptation. Raffles may need more than Holmes to keep him out of mischief. I am confident, however, that with you to watch out for me, I shall be able to suppress the strong tendency towards evil which at times besets me."

"We'd better keep out of it altogether, Holmes," said I, not liking the weight of responsibility for his good behavior that more than once he had placed on my shoulders. "You don't deny, I suppose, that the pearl rope is a factor in your intentions, whatever they may be."

"Of course I don't, Jenkins," was his response. "If it were not for her pearl rope, Mrs. Wilbraham Ward-Smythe could go anywhere she pleased without attracting any more attention from me than a passing motor-car. It would be futile for me to deny that, as a matter of fact, the pearl rope is an essent al part of my scheme, and, even if it were not futile to do so, I should still not deny it, because neither my father nor my grandfather, Holmes nor Raffles, ever forgot that a gentleman does not lie."

"Then count me out," said I.

"Even if there is $7500 in it for you?" he said, with a twinkle in his eye.

"If it were $107,500 you could still count me out," I retorted. "I don't like the business."

"Very well," said he, with a sigh. "I shall have to go alone and endeavor to fight the terrible temptation unaided, with a strong probability that I shall fail, and, yielding to it, commit my first real act of crime, and, in that event, with the possibility of a term at Trenton prison, if I am caught."

"Give it up, Raffles," I pleaded.

"And all because, in the hour of my need, my best friend, whose aid I begged, refused me," he went on, absolutely ignoring my plea.

"Oh, well, if you put it on that score," I said, "I'll go—but you must promise me not to touch the pearls."

"I'll do my best not to," he replied. "As usual, you have carte-blanche to put me out of business if you catch me trying it."

With this understanding I accompanied Raffles Holmes to Atlantic City the following afternoon, and the following evening we were registered at the Hotel Garrymore.

Holmes was not mistaken in his belief that Mrs. Wilbraham Ward-Smythe would take her famous pearl rope to Atlantic City with her. That very evening, while we were sitting at dinner, the lady entered, and draped about her stately neck and shoulders was the thing itself, and a more beautiful decoration was never

worn by woman from the days of the
Queen of Sheba to this day of lavish
display in jewels. It was a marvel,
indeed, but the moment I saw it I
ceased to give the lady credit for
superior virtue in failing to smuggle
it through the custom-house, for its
very size would have precluded the
possibility of a successful issue to any
such attempted evasion of the law.
It was too bulky to have been secreted
in any of the ordinary ways known
to smugglers. Hence her candid acknowledgment of its possession was
less an evidence of the lady's superior-
ity to the majority of her sex in the
matter of "beating the government"
than of her having been confronted
with the proverbial choice of the un-
identified Hobson.

"By Jove! Jenkins," Raffles Holmes
muttered, hoarsely, as Mrs. Ward-
Smythe paraded the length of the dining-room, as fairly corruscating with
her rich possessions as though she

were a jeweller's window incarnate,
"it's a positive crime for a woman to
appear in a place like this arrayed
like that. What right has she to
subject poor weak humanity to such
temptation as now confronts every
servant in this hotel, to say nothing
of guests, who, like ourselves, are
made breathless with such lavish
display? There's poor old Tommie
Bankson over there, for instance.
See how he gloats over those pearls.
He's fairly red-eyed over them."

I glanced across the dining-room,
and sure enough, there sat Tommie
Bankson, and even from where we
were placed we could see his hands
tremble with the itch for possession,
and his lips go dry with excitement
as he thought of the material assets
in full view under the glare of the
dining-room electric lights.

"I happen to know on the inside,"
continued Holmes, "that Tommie is
not only a virtual bankrupt through

stock speculation, but is actually face
to face with criminal disgrace for mis-
use of trust funds, all of which he
could escape if he could lay his hands
upon half the stuff that woman is so
carelessly wearing to-night. Do you
think it's fair to wear, for the mere
gratification of one's vanity, things
that arouse in the hearts of less fortunate beings such passionate reflections
and such dire temptations as those
which are now besetting that man?"

"I guess we've got enough to do
looking after Raffles to-night, old
man, without wasting any of our
nerve-tissue on Tommie Bankson," I
replied. "Come on—let's get out of
this. We'll go over to the Pentagon
for the night, and to-morrow we'll
shake the sands of Atlantic City from
our feet and hie ourselves back to
New York, where the temptations are
not so strong."

"It's too late," said Raffles Holmes.
"I've set out on this adventure and

I'm going to put it through. I wouldn't give up in the middle of an enterprise of this sort any more than I would let a balky horse refuse to take a fence I'd put him to. It's going to be harder than I thought, but we're in it, and I shall stay to the end."

"What the devil is the adventure, anyhow?" I demanded, impatiently. "You vowed you wouldn't touch the rope."

"I hope not to," was his response. "It is up to you to see that I don't. My plan does not involve my laying hands upon even the shadow of it."

So we stayed on at the Garrymore, and a worse week I never had anywhere. With every glimpse of that infernal jewel the Raffles in Holmes became harder and harder to control. In the daytime he was all right, but when night came on he was feverish with the desire to acquire possession of the pearls. Twice in the middle of the night I caught him endeavoring to sneak out of our room, and upon each occasion, when I rushed after him and forced him back, he made no denial of my charge that he was going after the jewel. The last time it involved us both in such a terrible struggle that I vowed then and there that the following morning should see my departure.

"I can't stand the strain, Holmes," said I.

"Well, if you can't stand *your* strain," said Raffles Holmes, "what do you think of mine?"

"The thing to do is to get out, that's all," I retorted. "I won't have a nerve left in twenty-four hours. For four nights now I haven't had a minute's normal sleep, and this fight you've just put up has regularly knocked me out."

"One more day Jenkins,' he pleaded. "She goes day after tomorrow, and so do we."

"We?" I cried. "After her?"

"Nope — she to Chicago — we to New York," said Holmes. "Stick it out, there's a good fellow," and of course I yielded.

The next day—Sunday—was one of feverish excitement, but we got through it without mishap, and on Monday morning it was with a sigh of relief that I saw Mrs. Wilbraham Ward-Smythe pull out of the Philadelphia station en route for Chicago, while Raffles Holmes and I returned to New York.

"Well, Raffles," said I, as we sped on our homeward way, "we've had our trouble for our pains."

He laughed crisply. "Have we?" said he. "I guess not—not unless you have lost the trunk check the porter gave you."

"What, this brass thing?" I demanded, taking the check from my pocket and flicking it in the air like a penny.

"I RUSHED AFTER HIM AND FORCED HIM BACK"

"That very brass thing," said Holmes.

"You haven't lifted that damned rope and put it in my trunk!" I roared.

"Hush, Jenkins! For Heaven's sake don't make a scene. I haven't done anything of the sort," he whispered, looking about him anxiously to make sure that we had not been overheard. "Those pearls are as innocent of my touch as the top of the Himalaya Mountains is of yours."

"Then what have you done?" I demanded, sulkily.

"Just changed a couple of trunk checks, that's all," said Raffles Holmes. "That bit of brass you have in your hand, which was handed to you in the station by the porter of the Garrymore, when presented at Jersey City will put you in possession of Mrs. Wilbraham Ward - Smythe's trunk, containing the bulk of her jewels. She's a trifle careless about her possessions, as any one could see who watched the nonchalant way in which she paraded the board walk with a small fortune on her neck and fingers. Most women would carry such things in a small hand-satchel, or at least have the trunk sent by registered express, but not Mrs. Wilbraham Ward-Smythe; and, thanks to her loud voice, listening outside of her door last night, I heard her directing her maid where she wished the gems packed."

"And where the dickens is my trunk?" I asked.

"On the way to Chicago," said Raffles Holmes, calmly. "Mrs. Wilbraham Ward-Smythe has the check for it."

"Safe business!" I sneered. "Bribed the porter, I presume?"

"Jenkins, you are exceedingly uncomplimentary at times," said Raffles Holmes, showing more resentment than I had ever given him credit for.

"Perhaps you observed that I didn't go to the station in the omnibus."

"No, you went over to the drug-store after some phenacetine for your headache," said I.

"Precisely," said Holmes, "and after purchasing the phenacetine I jumped aboard the Garrymore express-wagon and got a lift over to the station. It was during that ride that I transferred Mrs. Ward-Smythe's check from her trunk to yours, and vice versa. It's one of the easiest jobs in the Raffles business, especially at this season of the year, when travel is heavy and porters are over-worked."

"I'll see the trunk in the Hudson River, pearl rope and all, before I'll claim it at Jersey City or anywhere else," said I.

"Perfectly right," Holmes returned. "We'll hand the check to the expressman when he comes through the train, and neither of us need appear further in the matter. It will merely be delivered at your apartment."

"Why not yours?" said I.

"Raffles!" said he, laconically, and I understood.

"And then what?" I asked.

"Let it alone, unopened, safe as a church, until Mrs. Wilbraham Ward-Smythe discovers her loss, which will be to-morrow afternoon, and then—"

"Well?"

"Mr. Holmes will step in, unravel the mystery, prove it to be a mere innocent mistake, collect about ten or fifteen thousand dollars reward, divvy up with you, and the decks will be cleared for what turns up next," said this wonderful player of dangerous games. "And, as a beginning, Jenkins, please sign this," he added.

Holmes handed me a typewritten letter which read as follows:

The Brass Check

"THE RICHMORE, *June 30, 1905.*
"*Raffles Holmes, Esq..*

"DEAR SIR,—I enclose herewith my check for $1000 as a retainer for your services in locating for me a missing trunk, which contains articles which I value at $10,000. This trunk was checked through to New York from Atlantic City on Monday last, 9.40 train, and has not since been found. Whether or not it has been stolen, or has gone astray in some wholly innocent manner, is not as yet clear. I know of no one better equipped for the task of finding it for me than yourself, who, I am given to understand, are the son of the famous Sherlock Holmes of England. The check represents the ten per cent. commission on the value of the lost articles, which I believe is the customary fee for services such as I seek.   Very truly yours."

"What are you going to do with this?" I demanded.

"Send it as an enclosure to Mrs. Wilbraham Ward - Smythe, showing my credentials as your agent, in asking her if by any mischance your trunk has got mixed in with her luggage," observed Holmes. "For form's sake, I shall send it to twenty or thirty other people known to have left Atlantic City the same day. Moreover, it will suggest the idea to Mrs. Wilbraham Ward-Smythe that I am a good man to locate her trunk also, and the delicate intimation of my terms will—"

"Aha! I see," said I. "And my thousand-dollar check to you?"

"I shall, of course, keep," observed Holmes. "You want the whole business to be bona fide, don't you? It would be unscrupulous for you to ask for its return."

I didn't exactly like the idea, but, after all, there was much in what Holmes said, and the actual risk of my own capital relieved my conscience of the suspicion that by signing the letter I should become a partner in a confidence game. Hence I signed the note, mailed it to Raffles

Holmes, enclosing my check for $1000 with it.

Three days later Holmes entered my room with a broad grin on his face.

"How's this for business?" said he, handing me a letter he had received that morning from Chicago.

"DEAR SIR,—I am perfectly delighted to receive your letter of July 1. I think I have Mr. Jenkins's missing trunk. What pleases me most, however, is the possibility of your recovering mine, which also went astray at the same time. It contained articles of even greater value than Mr. Jenkins's—my pearl rope, among other things, which is appraised at $130,000. Do you think there is any chance of your recovering it for me? I enclose my check for $5000 as a retainer. The balance of your ten per cent. fee I shall gladly pay on receipt of my missing luggage.

"Most sincerely yours,
"MAUDE WARD-SMYTHE."

"I rather think, my dear Jenkins," observed Raffles Holmes, "that we have that $13,000 reward cinched."

R. Holmes & Co.

"There's $7000 for you, Jenkins," said Holmes, a week later, handing me his check for that amount. "Easy money that. It only took two weeks to turn the trick, and $14,000 for fourteen days' work is pretty fair pay. If we could count on that for a steady income I think I'd be able to hold Raffles down without your assistance.'

"You got fourteen thousand, eh?" said I. "I thought it was only to be $13,000."

"It was fourteen thousand counting in your $1000," said Raffles Holmes. "You see, I'm playing on the square, old man. Half and half in everything."

I squeezed his hand affectionately.

"But—he-ew!" I ejaculated, with a great feeling of relief. "I'm glad the thing's over with."

"So am I," said Holmes, with a glitter in his eye. "If we'd kept that trunk in this apartment another day there'd have been trouble. I had a piece of lead-pipe up my sleeve when I called here Tuesday night."

"What for?" I asked.

"You!" said Raffles Holmes. "If you hadn't had that poker-party with you I'd have knocked you out and gone to China with the Ward-Smythe jewels. Sherlock Holmes stock was 'way below par Tuesday night."

VI

THE ADVENTURE OF THE HIRED BURGLAR

I HAD not seen Raffles Holmes for some weeks, nor had I heard from him, although I had faithfully remitted to his address his share of the literary proceeds of his adventures as promptly as circumstances permitted —$600 on the first tale, $920 on the second, and no less than $1800 on the third, showing a constantly growing profit on our combination from my side of the venture. These checks had not even been presented for payment at the bank. Fearing from this that he might be ill, I called at Holmes's lodgings in the Rexmere, a well-established bachelor apartment

The Hired Burglar

hotel, on Forty-fourth Street, to inquire as to the state of his health. The clerk behind the desk greeted me cordially as I entered, and bade me go at once to Holmes's apartment on the eighteenth floor, which I immediately proceeded to do.

"Here is Mr. Holmes's latch-key, sir," said the clerk. "He told me you were to have access to his apartment at any time."

"He is in, is he?" I asked.

"I really don't know, sir. I will call up and inquire, if you wish," replied the clerk.

"Oh, never mind," said I. "I'll go up, anyhow, and if he is out, I'll wait."

So up I went, and a few moments later had entered the apartment. As the door opened, the little private hallway leading to his den at the rear burst into a flood of light, and from an inner room, the entrance to which was closed, I could hear Holmes's

voice cheerily carolling out snatches
of such popular airs as "Tammany"
and "Ef Yo' Habn't Got No Money
Yo' Needn't Bodder Me."

I laughed quietly and at the same
time breathed a sigh of relief. It was
very evident from the tone of his
voice that there was nothing serious
the matter with my friend and
partner.

"Hullo, Raffles!" I called out,
knocking on the door to the inner
room.

> *"Tam-ma-nee, Tam-ma-nee;*
> *Swampum, swampum,*
> *Get their wampum,*
> *Tam-ma-nee,"*

was the sole answer, and in such
fortissimo tones that I was not sur-
prised that he did not hear me.

"Oh, I say, Raffles," I hallooed,
rapping on the door again, this time
with the head of my cane. "It's
Jenkins, old man. Came to look you

up. Was afraid something had happened to you."

> "'*Way down upon the Suwanee River,*
> *Far, far away,*
> *Dere's whar my heart am turnin' ever,*
> *Dere's whar de ole folks stay,*"

was the reply.

Again I laughed.

"He's suffering from a bad attack of coonitis this evening," I observed to myself. "Looks to me as if I'd have to let it run its course."

Whereupon I retired to a very comfortable couch near the window and sat down to await the termination of the musical.

Five minutes later the singing having shown no signs of abatement I became impatient, and a third assault on the door followed, this time with cane, hands, and toes in unison.

"I'll have him out this time or die!" I ejaculated, filled with resolve, and then began such a pounding upon the door as should have sufficed to awake a dead Raffles, not to mention a living one.

"Hi, there, Jenkins!" cried a voice behind me, in the midst of this operation, identically the same voice, too, as that still going on in the room in front of me. "What the dickens are you trying to do—batter the house down?"

I whirled about like a flash, and was deeply startled to see Raffles himself standing by the divan I had just vacated, divesting himself of his gloves and light overcoat.

"You—Raffles?" I roared in astonishment.

"Yep," said he. "Who else?"

"But the—the other chap—in the room there?"

"Oh," laughed Raffles. "That's my alibi-prover—hold on a minute and I'll show you."

Whereupon he unlocked the door into the bedroom, whence had come the tuneful lyrics, threw it wide open, and revealed to my astonished gaze no less an object than a large talking-machine still engaged in the strenuous fulfilment of its noisy mission.

"What the dickens!" I said.

"It's attached to my front-door," said Raffles, silencing the machine. "The minute the door is opened it begins to sing like the four - and - twenty blackbirds baked in a pie."

"But what good is it?" said I.

"Oh, well—it keeps the servants from spending too much time in my apartment, snooping among my papers, perhaps; and it may some day come in useful in establishing an alibi if things go wrong with me. You'd have sworn I was in there just now, wouldn't you?"

"I would indeed," said I.

"Well—you see, I wasn't, so there you are," said Raffles Holmes. "By-the-way, you've come at an interesting moment. There'll be things do-

ing before the evening is over. I've
had an anxious caller here five times
already to-day. I've been standing
in the barber-shop opposite getting
a line on him. His card name is
Grouch, his real name is—"

Here Raffles Holmes leaned for-
ward and whispered in my ear a
name of such eminent respectability
that I fairly gasped.

"You don't mean *the* Mr. ——"

"Nobody else," said Raffles Holmes.
"Only he don't know I know who he
is. The third time Grouch called I
trailed him to Blank's house, and
then recognized him as Blank himself."

"And what does he want with
you?" I asked.

"That remains to be seen," said
Raffles Holmes. "All I know is that
next Tuesday he will be required to
turn over $100,000 unregistered bonds
to a young man about to come of age,
for whom he has been a trustee."

The Hired Burglar

"Aha!" said I. "And you think—"

"I don't think, Jenkins, until the time comes. Gray matter is scarce these times, and I'm not wasting any of mine on unnecessary speculation," said Raffles Holmes.

At this point the telephone-bell rang and Raffles answered the summons.

"Yes, I'll see Mr. Grouch. Show him up," he said. "It would be mighty interesting reading if some newspaper showed him up," he added, with a grin, as he returned. "By-the-way, Jenkins, I think you'd better go in there and have a half-hour's chat with the talking-machine. I have an idea old man Grouch won't have much to say with a third party present. Listen all you want to, but don't breathe too loud or you'll frighten him away."

I immediately retired, and a moment later Mr. Grouch entered Raffles Holmes's den.

"Glad to see you," said Raffles Holmes, cordially. "I was wondering how soon you'd be here."

"You expected me, then?" asked the visitor, in surprise.

"Yes," said Holmes. "Next Tuesday is young Wilbraham's twenty-first birthday, and—"

Peering through a crack in the door I could see Grouch stagger.

"You — you know my errand, then?" he gasped out.

"Only roughly, Mr. Grouch," said Holmes, coolly. "Only roughly. But I am very much afraid that I can't do what you want me to. Those bonds are doubtless in some broker's box in a safe-deposit company, and I don't propose to try to borrow them surreptitiously, even temporarily, from an incorporated institution. It is not only a dangerous but a criminal operation. Does your employer know that you have taken them?"

The Hired Burglar

"My employer?" stammered Grouch, taken off his guard.

"Yes. Aren't you the confidential secretary of Mr. ——?" Here Holmes mentioned the name of the eminent financier and philanthropist. No one would have suspected, from the tone of his voice, that Holmes was perfectly aware that Grouch and the eminent financier were one and the same person. The idea seemed to please and steady the visitor.

"Why—ah—yes—I am Mr. Blank's confidential secretary," he blurted out. "And—ah—of course Mr. Blank does not know that I have speculated with the bonds and lost them."

"The bonds are—"

"In the hands of Bunker & Burke. I had hoped you would be able to suggest some way in which I could get hold of them long enough to turn them over to young Wilbraham, and then, in some other way, to restore them later to Bunker & Burke."

"That is impossible," said Raffles Holmes. "For the reasons stated, I cannot be a party to a criminal operation."

"It will mean ruin for me if it cannot be done," moaned Grouch. "For Mr. Blank as well, Mr. Holmes; he is so deep in the market he can't possibly pull out. I thought possibly you knew of some reformed cracksman who would do this one favor for me just to tide things over. All we need is three weeks' time—three miserable little weeks."

"Can't be done with a safe-deposit company at the other end of the line," said Raffles Holmes. "If it were Mr. Blank's own private vault at his home it would be different. That would be a matter between gentlemen, between Mr. Blank and myself, but the other would put a corporation on the trail of the safe-breaker—an uncompromising situation."

Grouch's eye glistened.

The Hired Burglar

"You know a man who, for a consideration and with a guarantee against prosecution, would break open my — I mean Mr. Blank's private vault?" he cried.

"I think so," said Raffles Holmes, noncommittally. "Not as a crime, however, merely as a favor, and with the lofty purpose of saving an honored name from ruin. My advice to you would be to put a dummy package, supposed to contain the missing bonds, along with about $30,000 worth of other securities in that vault, and so arrange matters that on the night preceding the date of young Wilbraham's majority, the man I will send you shall have the opportunity to crack it open and get away with the stuff unmolested and unseen. Next day young Wilbraham will see for himself why it is that Mr. Blank cannot turn over his trust. That is the only secure and I may say decently honest way out of your trouble."

"Mr. Raffles Holmes, you are a genius!" cried Grouch, ecstatically. And then he calmed down again as an unpleasant thought flashed across his mind. "Why is it necessary to put $30,000 additional in the safe, Mr. Holmes?"

"Simply as a blind," said Holmes. "Young Wilbraham would be suspicious if the burglar got away with nothing but his property, wouldn't he?"

"Quite so," said Grouch. "And now, Mr. Holmes, what will this service cost me?"

"Five thousand dollars," said Holmes.

"Phe-e-e-w!" whistled Grouch. "Isn't that pretty steep?"

"No, Mr. Grouch. I save two reputations—yours and Mr. Blank's. Twenty-five hundred dollars is not much to pay for a reputation these days—I mean a real one, of course, such as yours is up to date," said Holmes, coldly.

The Hired Burglar

"Payable by certified check?" said Grouch.

"Not much," laughed Holmes. "In twenty-dollar bills, Mr. Grouch. You may leave them in the safe along with the other valuables."

"Thank you, Mr. Holmes," said Grouch, rising. "It shall be as you say. Before I go, sir, may I ask how you knew me and by what principle of deduction you came to guess my business so accurately?"

"It was simple enough," said Holmes. "I knew, in the first place, that so eminent a person as Mr. Blank would not come to me in the guise of a Mr. Grouch if he hadn't some very serious trouble on his mind. I knew, from reading the society items in the *Whirald*, that Mr. Bobby Wilbraham would celebrate the attainment of his majority by a big fête on the 17th of next month. Everybody knows that Mr. Blank is Mr. Wilbraham's trustee until he comes of age. It was easy enough to surmise from that what the nature of the trouble was. Two and two almost invariably make four, Mr. Grouch."

"And how the devil," demanded Grouch, angrily—"how the devil did you know I was Blank?"

"Mr. Blank passes the plate at the church I go to every Sunday," said Holmes, laughing, "and it would take a great sight more than a two-dollar wig and a pair of fifty-cent whiskers to conceal that pompous manner of his."

"Tush! You would better not make me angry, Mr. Holmes," said Grouch, reddening.

"You can get as angry as you think you can afford to, for all I care, Mr. Blank," said Holmes. "It's none of my funeral, you know."

And so the matter was settled. The unmasked Blank, seeing that wrath was useless, calmed down and

The Hired Burglar

accepted Holmes's terms and method for his relief.

"I'll have my man there at 4 A.M., October 17th, Mr. Blank," said Holmes. "See that your end of it is ready. The coast must be kept clear or the scheme falls through."

Grouch went heavily out, and Holmes called me back into the room.

"Jenkins," said he, "that man is one of the biggest scoundrels in creation, and I'm going to give him a jolt."

"Where are you going to get the retired burglar?" I asked.

"Sir," returned Raffles Holmes, "this is to be a personally conducted enterprise. It's a job worthy of my grandsire on my mother's side. Raffles will turn the trick."

And it turned out so to be, for the affair went through without a hitch. The night of October 16th I spent at Raffles's apartments. He was as

...m as though nothing unusual were on hand. He sang songs, played the piano, and up to midnight was as gay and skittish as a school-boy on vacation. As twelve o'clock struck, however, he sobered down, put on his hat and coat, and, bidding me remain where I was, departed by means of the fire-escape.

"Keep up the talk, Jenkins," he said. "The walls are thin here, and it's just as well, in matters of this sort, that our neighbors should have the impression that I have *not* gone out. I've filled the machine up with a choice lot of songs and small-talk to take care of my end of it. A consolidated gas company, like yourself, should have no difficulty in filling in the gaps."

And with that he left me to as merry and withal as nervous a three hours as I ever spent in my life. Raffles had indeed filled that talking-machine—thirteen full cylinders of it

The Hired Burglar

—with as choice an assortment of *causerie* and humorous anecdotes as any one could have wished to hear. Now and again it would bid me cheer up and not worry about him. Once, along about 2 A.M., it cried out: "You ought to see me now, Jenkins. I'm right in the middle of this Grouch job, and it's a dandy. I'll teach *him* a lesson." The effect of all this was most uncanny. It was as if Raffles Holmes himself spoke to me from the depths of that dark room in the Blank household, where he was engaged in an enterprise of dreadful risk merely to save the good name of one who no longer deserved to bear such a thing. In spite of all this, however, as the hours passed I began to grow more and more nervous. The talking-machine sang and chattered, but when four o'clock came and Holmes had not yet returned, I became almost frenzied with excitement — and then at the climax of the tension came the flash of his dark-lantern on the fire-escape, and he climbed heavily into the room.

"Thank Heaven you're back," I cried.

"You have reason to," said Holmes, sinking into a chair. "Give me some whiskey. That man Blank is a worse scoundrel than I took him for."

"What's happened?" I asked. "Didn't he play square?"

"No," said Holmes, breathing heavily. "He waited until I had busted the thing open and was on my way out in the dark hall, and then pounced on me with his butler and valet. I bowled the butler down the kitchen stairs, and sent the valet howling into the dining-room with an appendicitis jab in the stomach, and had the pleasure of blacking both of Mr. Blank's eyes."

"And the stuff?"

"Right here," said Holmes, tapping his chest. "I was afraid something

"'I SENT THE VALET HOWLING INTO THE DINING-
ROOM . . . AND HAD THE PLEASURE OF BLACKING
BOTH OF MR. BLANK'S EYES'"

The Hired Burglar

might happen on the way out and I kept both hands free. I haven't much confidence in philanthropists like Blank. Fortunately the scrimmage was in the dark, so Blank will never know who hit him."

"What are you going to do with the $35,000?" I queried, as we went over the booty later and found it all there.

"Don't know—haven't made up my mind," said Holmes, laconically. "I'm too tired to think about that now. It's me for bed." And with that he turned in.

Two days later, about nine o'clock in the evening, Mr. Grouch again called, and Holmes received him courteously.

"Well, Mr. Holmes," Grouch observed, unctuously, rubbing his hands together, "it was a nice job, neatly done. It saved the day for me. Wilbraham was satisfied, and has given me a whole year to make good the loss. My reputation is saved, and—"

"Excuse me, Mr. Blank—or Grouch —er—to what do you refer?" asked Holmes.

"Why, our little transaction of Monday night—or was it Tuesday morning?" said Grouch.

"Oh—that!" said Holmes. "Well, I'm glad to hear you managed to pull it off satisfactorily. I was a little worried about it. I was afraid you were done for."

"Done for?" said Grouch. "No, indeed. The little plan went off without a hitch."

"Good," said Holmes. "I congratulate you. *Whom did you get to do the job?*"

"Who—what—what—why, what do you mean, Mr. Holmes?" gasped Grouch.

"Precisely what I say—or maybe you don't like to tell me—such things are apt to be on a confidential basis.

The Hired Burglar

Anyhow, I'm glad you're safe, Mr. Grouch, and I hope your troubles are over."

"They will be when you give me back my $30,000," said Grouch.

"Your what?" demanded Holmes, with well-feigned surprise.

"My $30,000," repeated Blank, his voice rising to a shout.

"My dear Mr. Grouch," said Holmes, "how should I know anything about your $30,000?"

"Didn't your—your man take it?" demanded Grouch, huskily.

"My man? Really, Mr. Grouch, you speak in riddles this evening. Pray make yourself more clear."

"Your reformed burglar, who broke open my safe, and—" Grouch went on.

"I have no such man, Mr. Grouch."

"Didn't you send a man to my house, Mr. Raffles, to break open my safe, and take certain specified parcels of negotiable property therefrom?" said Grouch, rising and pounding the table with his fists.

"*I did not!*" returned Holmes, with equal emphasis. "I have never in my life sent anybody to your house, sir."

"Then who in the name of Heaven did?" roared Grouch. "The stuff is gone."

Holmes shrugged his shoulders.

"I am willing," said he, calmly, "to undertake to find out who did it, if anybody, if that is what you mean, Mr. Grouch. Ferreting out crime is my profession. Otherwise, I beg to assure you that my interest in the case ceases at this moment."

Here Holmes rose with quiet dignity and walked to the door.

"You will find me at my office in the morning, Mr. Grouch," he remarked, "in case you wish to consult me professionally."

"Hah!" sneered Grouch. "You think you can put me off this way, do you?"

The Hired Burglar

"I think so," said Holmes, with a glittering eye. "No gentleman or other person may try to raise a disturbance in my private apartments and remain there."

"We'll see what the police have to say about this, Mr. Raffles Holmes," Grouch shrieked, as he made for the door.

"Very well," said Holmes. "I've no doubt they will find our discussion of the other sinners very interesting. They are welcome to the whole story as far as I am concerned."

And he closed the door on the ashen face of the suffering Mr. Grouch.

"What shall I do with your share of the $30,000, Jenkins?" said Raffles Holmes a week later.

"Anything you please," said I. "Only don't offer any of it to me. I can't question the abstract justice of your mulcting old Blank for the amount, but, somehow or other, I don't want any of it myself. Send it to the Board of Foreign Missions."

"Good!" said Holmes. "That's what I've done with my share. See!"

And he showed me an evening paper in which the board conveyed its acknowledgment of the generosity of an unknown donor of the princely sum of $15,000.

VII

THE REDEMPTION OF YOUNG BILLING-
TON RAND

"JENKINS," said Raffles Holmes,
lighting his pipe and throwing
himself down upon my couch, "don't
you sometimes pine for those good
old days of Jack Sheppard and Dick
Turpin? Hang it all—I'm getting
blisteringly tired of the modern re-
finements in crime, and yearn for the
period when the highwayman met
you on the road and made you stand
and deliver at the point of the
pistol."

"Indeed I don't!" I ejaculated.
"I'm not chicken-livered, Raffles,
but I'm mighty glad my lines are

ıst in less strenuous scenes. When a book-agent comes in here, for instance, and holds me up for nineteen dollars a volume for a set of Kipling in words of one syllable, illustrated by his aunt, and every volume autographed by his uncle's step-sister, it's a game of wits between us as to whether I shall buy or not buy, and if he gets away with my signature to a contract it is because he has legitimately outwitted me. But your ancient Turpin overcame you by brute force; you hadn't a run for your money from the moment he got his eye on you, and no percentage of the swag was ever returned to you as in the case of the Double-Cross Edition of Kipling, in which you get at least fifty cents worth of paper and print for every nineteen dollars you give up."

"That is merely the commercial way of looking at it," protested Holmes. "You reckon up the situa-

tion on a basis of mere dollars, strike
a balance and charge the thing up to
profit and loss. But the romance of
it all, the element of the picturesque,
the delicious, tingling sense of adventure which was inseparable from
a road experience with a commanding
personality like Turpin—these things
are all lost in your prosaic book-agent
methods of our day. No man writing his memoirs for the enlightenment
of posterity would ever dream of
setting down upon paper the story of
how a book-agent robbed him of two
hundred dollars, but the chap who
has been held up in the dark recesses
of a forest on a foggy night by a Jack
Sheppard would always find breathless and eager listeners to or readers of
the tale he had to tell, even if he lost
only a nickel by the transaction."

"Well, old man," said I, "I'm
satisfied with the prosaic methods of
the gas companies, the book-agents,
and the riggers of the stock-market.

R. Holmes & Co.

Give me Wall Street and you take Dick Turpin and all his crew. But what has set your mind to working on the Dick Turpin end of it anyhow? Thinking of going in for that sort of thing yourself?"

"M-m-m yes," replied Holmes, hesitatingly. "I am. Not that I pine to become one of the Broom Squires myself, but because I—well, I may be forced into it."

"Take my advice, Raffles," I interrupted, earnestly. "Let fire-arms and highways alone. There's too much of battle, murder, and sudden death in loaded guns, and a surplus of publicity in street work."

"You mustn't take me so literally, Jenkins," he retorted. "I'm not going to follow precisely in the steps of Turpin, but a hold-up on the public highway seems to be the only way out of a problem which I have been employed to settle. Do you know young Billington Rand?"

Redemption of Young Rand

"By sight," said I, with a laugh. "And by reputation. You're not going to hold him up, are you?" I added, contemptuously.

"Why not?" said Holmes.

"It's like breaking into an empty house in search of antique furniture," I explained. "Common report has it that Billington Rand has already been skinned by about every skinning agency in town. He's posted at all his clubs. Every gambler in town, professional as well as social, has his I.O.U.'s for bridge, poker, and faro debts. Everybody knows it except those fatuous people down in the Kenesaw National Bank, where he's employed, and the Fidelity Company that's on his bond. He wouldn't last five minutes in either place if his uncle wasn't a director in both concerns."

"I see that you have a pretty fair idea of Billington Rand's financial condition," said Holmes.

"It's rather common talk in the clubs, so why shouldn't I?" I put in. "Holding him up would be at most an act of petit larceny, if you measure a crime by what you get out of it. It's a great shame, though, for at heart Rand is one of the best fellows in the world. He's a man who has all the modern false notions of what a fellow ought to do to keep up what he calls his end. He plays cards and sustains ruinous losses because he thinks he won't be considered a good-fellow if he stays out. He plays bridge with ladies and pays up when he loses and doesn't collect when he wins. Win or lose he's doomed to be on the wrong side of the market just because of those very qualities that make him a lovable person—kind to everybody but himself, and weak as dish-water. For Heaven's sake, Raffles, if the poor devil *has* anything left don't take it from him."

"Your sympathy for Rand does

you credit," said Holmes. "But I have just as much of that as you have, and that is why, at half-past five o'clock to-morrow afternoon, I'm going to hold him up, in the public eye, and incontinently rob him of $25,000."

"Twenty-five thousand dollars? Billington Rand?" I gasped.

"Twenty-five thousand dollars. Billington Rand," repeated Holmes, firmly. "If you don't believe it come along and see. He doesn't know you, does he?"

"Not from Adam," said I.

"Very good—then you'll be safe as a church. Meet me in the Fifth Avenue Hotel corridor at five to-morrow afternoon and I'll show you as pretty a hold-up as you ever dreamed of," said Holmes.

"But—I can't take part in a criminal proceeding like that, Holmes," I protested.

"You won't have to—even if it

were a criminal proceeding, which it is not," he returned. "Nobody outside of you and me will know anything about it but Rand himself, and the chances that he will peach are less than a millionth part of a half per cent. Anyhow, all you need be is a witness."

There was a long and uneasy silence. I was far from liking the job, but after all, so far, Holmes had not led me into any difficulties of a serious nature, and, knowing him as I had come to know him, I had a hearty belief that any wrong he did was temporary and was sure to be rectified in the long run.

"I've a decent motive in all this, Jenkins," he resumed in a few moments. "Don't forget that. This hold-up is going to result in a reformation that will be for the good of everybody, so don't have any scruples on that score."

"All right, Raffles," said I. "You've

always played straight with me, so far, and I don't doubt your word—only I hate the highway end of it."

"Tutt, Jenkins!" he ejaculated, with a laugh and giving me a whack on the shoulders that nearly toppled me over into the fire-place. "Don't be a rabbit. The thing will be as easy as cutting calve's-foot jelly with a razor."

Thus did I permit myself to be persuaded, and the next afternoon at five, Holmes and I met in the corridor of the Fifth Avenue Hotel.

"Come on," he said, after the first salutations were over. "Rand will be at the Thirty-third Street subway at 5.15, and it is important that we should catch him before he gets to Fifth Avenue."

"I'm glad it's to be on a side street," I remarked, my heart beating rapidly with excitement over the work in hand, for the more I thought of the venture the less I liked it.

"Oh, I don't know that it will be," said Holmes, carelessly. "I may pull it off in the corridors of the Powhatan."

The pumps in my heart reversed their action and for a moment I feared I should drop with dismay.

"In the Powhatan—" I began.

"Shut up, Jenkins!" said Holmes, imperatively. "This is no time for protests. We're in it now and there's no drawing back."

Ten minutes later we stood at the intersection of Thirty-third Street and Fifth Avenue. Holmes's eyes flashed and his whole nervous system quivered as with the joy of the chase.

"Keep your mouth shut, Jenkins, and you'll see a pretty sight," he whispered, "for here comes our man."

Sure enough, there was Billington Rand on the other side of the street, walking along nervously and clutching an oblong package, wrapped in brown paper, firmly in his right hand.

Redemption of Young Rand

"Now for it," said Holmes, and we crossed the street, scarcely reaching the opposite curb before Rand was upon us. Rand eyed us closely and shied off to one side as Holmes blocked his progress.

"I'll trouble you for that package, Mr. Rand," said Holmes, quietly.

The man's face went white and he caught his breath.

"Who the devil are you?" he demanded, angrily.

"That has nothing to do with the case," retorted Holmes. "I want that package or—"

"Get out of my way!" cried Rand, with a justifiable show of resentment. "Or I'll call an officer."

"Will you?" said Holmes, quietly. "Will you call an officer and so make known to the authorities that you are in possession of twenty-five thousand dollars worth of securities that belong to other people, which are supposed at this moment to be safely locked up in the vaults of the Kene-saw National Bank along with other collateral?"

Rand staggered back against the newel-post of a brown-stone stoop, and stood there gazing wildly into Holmes's face.

"Of course, if you prefer having the facts made known in that way," Holmes continued, coolly, "you have the option. I am not going to use physical force to persuade you to hand the package over to me, but you are a greater fool than I take you for if you choose that alternative. To use an expressive modern phrase, Mr. Billington Rand, you will be caught with the goods on, and unless you have a far better explanation of how those securities happen in your pos-session at this moment than I think you have, there is no power on earth can keep you from landing in state-prison."

The unfortunate victim of Holmes's

adventure fairly gasped in his combined rage and fright. Twice he attempted to speak, but only inarticulate sounds issued from his lips.

"You are, of course, very much disturbed at the moment," Holmes went on, "and I am really very sorry if anything I have done has disarranged any honorable enterprise in which you have embarked. I don't wish to hurry you into a snap decision, which you may repent later, only either the police or I must have that package within an hour. It is for you to say which of us is to get it. Suppose we run over to the Powhatan and discuss the matter calmly over a bottle of Glengarry? Possibly I can convince you that it will be for your own good to do precisely as I tell you and very much to your disadvantage to do otherwise."

Rand, stupefied by this sudden intrusion upon his secret by an utter stranger, lost what little fight there

was left in him, and at least seemed
to assent to Holmes's proposition.
The latter linked arms with him, and
in a few minutes we walked into the
famous hostelry just as if we were
three friends, bent only upon having a pleasant chat over a café
table.

"What 'll you have, Mr. Rand?"
asked Holmes, suavely. "I'm elect-
ed for the Glengarry special, with a
little carbonic on the side."

"Same," said Rand, laconically.

"Sandwich with it?" asked Holmes.
"You'd better."

"Oh, I can't eat anything," began
Rand. "I—"

"Bring us some sandwiches, waiter,
said Holmes. "Two Glengarry special, a syphon of carbonic, and—
Jenkins, what's yours?"

The calmness and the cheek of the
fellow!

"I'm not in on this at all," I retorted, angered by Holmes's use of

my name. "And I want Mr. Rand
to understand—"

"Oh, tutt!" ejaculated Holmes. "*He*
knows that. Mr. Rand, my friend
Jenkins has no connection with this
enterprise of mine, and he's done his
level best to dissuade me from holding you up so summarily. All he's
along for is to write the thing up
for—"

"The newspapers?" cried Rand,
now thoroughly frightened.

"No," laughed Holmes. "Nothing
so useful—the magazines."

Holmes winked at me as he spoke,
and I gathered that there was method
in his apparent madness.

"That's one of the points you want
to consider, though, Mr. Rand," he
said, leaning upon the table with his
elbows. "Think of the newspapers
to-morrow morning if you call the
police rather than hand that package
over to me. It 'll be a big sensation
for Wall Street and upper Fifth

Avenue, to say nothing of what the yellows will make of the story for the rest of hoi polloi. The newsboys will be yelling extras all over town, printed in great, red letters, 'A Clubman Held-Up In Broad Daylight, For $25,000 In Securities That Didn't Belong to Him. Billington Rand Has Something To Explain. Where Did He Get It?—"

"For Heavens sake, man! don't!" pleaded the unfortunate Billington. "God! I never thought of that."

"Of course you didn't think of that," said Holmes. "That's why I'm telling you about it now. You don't dispute my facts, do you?"

"No, I—" Rand began.

"Of course not," said Holmes. "You might as well dispute the existence of the Flat-iron Building. If you don't want to-morrow's papers to be full of this thing you'll hand that package over to me."

"But," protested Rand, "I'm only

taking them up to—to a—er—to a
broker." Here he gathered himself
together and spoke with greater
assurance. "I am delivering them,
sir, to a broker, on behalf of one of
our depositors who—"

"Who has been speculating with
what little money he had left, has
lost his margins, and is now forced
into an act of crime to protect
his speculation," said Holmes. "The
broker is the notorious William C.
Gallagher, who runs an up-town
bucket-shop for speculative ladies to
lose their pin-money and bridge win-
nings in, and your depositor's name
is Billington Rand, Esq.—otherwise
yourself."

"How do you know all this?"
gasped Rand.

"Oh—maybe I read it on the
ticker," laughed Holmes. "Or, what
is more likely, possibly I overheard
Gallagher recommending you to dip
into the bank's collateral to save

your investment, at Green's chop-house last night."

"You were at Green's chop-house last night?" cried Rand.

"In the booth adjoining your own, and I heard every word you said," said Holmes.

"Well, I don't see why I should give the stuff to you anyhow," growled Rand.

"Chiefly because I happen to be long on information which would be of interest, not only to the police, but to the president and board of directors of the Kenesaw National Bank, Mr. Rand," said Holmes. "It will be a simple matter for me to telephone Mr. Horace Huntington, the president of your institution, and put him wise to this transaction of yours, and that is the second thing I shall do immediately you have decided not to part with that package."

"The second thing?" Rand whimpered. "What will you do first?"

"Communicate with the first policeman we meet when we leave here," said Holmes. "But take your time, Mr. Rand—take your time. Don't let me hurry you into a decision. Try a little of this Glengarry and we'll drink hearty to a sensible conclusion."

"I — I'll put them back in the vaults to-morrow," pleaded Rand.

"Can't trust you, my boy," said Holmes. "Not with a persuasive crook like old Bucket-shop Gallagher on your trail. They're safer with me."

Rand's answer was a muttered oath as he tossed the package across the table and started to leave us.

"One word more, Mr. Rand," said Holmes, detaining him. "Don't do anything rash. There's a lot of good-fellowship between criminals, and I'll stand by you all right. So far nobody knows you took these things, and even when they turn up missing, if you go about your work as if nothing had happened, while you may be suspected, nobody can *prove* that you got the goods."

Rand's face brightened at this remark.

"By Jove!—that's true enough," said he. "Except Gallagher," he added, his face falling.

"Pah for Gallagher!" cried Holmes, snapping his fingers contemptuously. "If he as much as peeped we could put him in jail, and if he sells you out you tell him for me that I'll land him in Sing Sing for a term of years. He led you into this—"

"He certainly did," moaned Rand.

"And he's got to get you out," said Holmes. "Now, good-bye, old man. The worst that can happen to you is a few judgments instead of penal servitude for eight or ten years, unless you are foolish enough to try another turn of this sort, and then you may not happen on a good-natured highwayman like myself to get you out of your troubles. By-the-way, what is the combination of the big safe in the outer office of the Kenesaw National?"

"One-eight-nine-seven," said Rand.

"Thanks," said Holmes, jotting it down coolly in his memorandum-book. "That's a good thing to know."

That night, shortly before mid-night, Holmes left me. "I've got to finish this job," said he. "The most ticklish part of the business is yet to come."

"Great Scott, Holmes!" I cried. "Isn't the thing done?"

"No—of course not," he replied. "I've got to bust open the Kenesaw safe."

"Now, my dear Raffles," I began, "why aren't you satisfied with what you've done already. Why must you—"

"Shut up, Jenkins," he interrupted,

with a laugh. "If you knew what I was going to do you wouldn't kick—that is, unless you've turned crook too?"

"Not I," said I, indignantly.

"You don't expect me to keep these bonds, do you?" he asked.

"But what are you going to do with them?" I retorted.

"Put 'em back in the Kenesaw Bank, where they belong, so that they'll be found there to-morrow morning. As sure as I don't, Billington Rand is doomed," said he. "It's a tough job, but I've been paid a thousand dollars by his family, to find out what he's up to, and by thunder, after following his trail for three weeks, I've got such a liking for the boy that I'm going to save him if it can be done, and if there's any Raffles left in me, such a simple proposition as cracking a bank and puting the stuff back where it belongs, in a safe of which I have the combination, isn't going to stand in my way. Don't fret, old man, it's as good as done. Good-night."

And Raffles Holmes was off. I passed a feverish night, but at five o'clock the following morning a telephone message set all my misgivings at rest.

"Hello, Jenkins!" came Raffles's voice over the wire.

"Hello," I replied.

"Just rang you up to let you know that it's all right. The stuff's replaced. Easiest job ever—like opening oysters. Pleasant dreams to you," he said, and, click, the connection was broken.

Two weeks later Billington Rand resigned from the Kenesaw Bank and went West, where he is now leading the simple life on a sheep-ranch. His resignation was accepted with regret, and the board of directors, as a special mark of their liking, voted him a gift of $2500 for faithful services.

"And the best part of it was," said Holmes, when he told me of the young man's good fortune, "that his accounts were as straight as a string."

"Holmes, you are a bully chap!" I cried, in a sudden excess of enthusiasm. "You do things for nothing sometimes—"

"Nothing!" echoed Holmes—"nothing! Why, that job was worth a million dollars to me, Jenkins—but not in coin. Just in good solid satisfaction in saving a fine young chap like Billington Rand from the clutches of a sharper and sneaking skinflint like old Bucket-shop Gallagher."

VIII

"THE NOSTALGIA OF NERVY JIM THE
SNATCHER"

RAFFLES HOLMES was unusu-
ally thoughtful the other night
when he entered my apartment, and
for a long time I could get nothing
out of him save an occasional grunt
of assent or dissent from propositions
advanced by myself. It was quite
evident that he was cogitating deeply
over some problem that was more than
ordinarily vexatious, so I finally gave
up all efforts at conversation, pushed
the cigars closer to him, poured him
out a stiff dose of his favorite Glengarry, and returned to my own work.
It was a full hour before he volun-

159

teered an observation of any kind, and then he plunged rapidly into a very remarkable tale.

"I had a singular adventure to-day, Jenkins," he said. "Do you happen to have in your set of my father's adventures a portrait of Sherlock Holmes?"

"Yes, I have," I replied. "But you don't need anything of the kind to refresh your memory of him. All you have to do is to look at yourself in the glass, and you've got the photograph before you."

"I *am* so like him then?" he queried.

"Most of the time, old man, I am glad to say," said I. "There are days when you are the living image of your grandfather Raffles, but that is only when you are planning some scheme of villany. I can almost invariably detect the trend of your thoughts by a glance at your face — you are Holmes himself in your honest moments, Raffles at others. For the past week it has delighted me more than I can say to find you a fac-simile of your splendid father, with naught to suggest your fascinating but vicious granddad."

"That's what I wanted to find out. I had evidence of it this afternoon on Broadway," said he. "It was bitterly cold up around Fortieth Street, snowing like the devil, and such winds as you'd expect to find nowhere this side of Greenland's icy mountains. I came out of a Broadway chop-house and started north, when I was stopped by an ill-clad, down-trodden specimen of humanity, who begged me, for the love of Heaven to give him a drink. The poor chap's condition was such that it would have been manslaughter to refuse him, and a moment later I had him before the Skidmore bar, gurgling down a tumblerful of raw brandy as though it were water. He wiped his mouth on his sleeve and turned to thank me, when a look of recognition came into his face, and he staggered back half in fear and half in amazement.

"'Sherlock Holmes!' he cried.

"'Am I?' said I, calmly, my curiosity much excited.

"'Him or his twin!' said he.

"'How should you know me?' I asked.

"'Good reason enough,' he muttered. ''Twas Sherlock Holmes as landed me for ten years in Reading gaol.'

"'Well, my friend,' I answered, 'I've no doubt you deserved it if he did it. I am *not* Sherlock Holmes, however, but his son.'

"'Will you let me take you by the hand, governor?' he whispered, hoarsely. 'Not for the kindness you've shown me here, but for the service your old man did me. I am Nervy Jim the Snatcher.'

"'Service?' said I, with a laugh.

"Nostalgia of Nervy Jim"

'You consider it a service to be landed in Reading gaol?'

"'They was the only happy years I ever had, sir,' he answered, impetuously. 'The keepers was good to me. I was well fed; kept workin' hard at an honest job, pickin' oakum; the gaol was warm, and I never went to bed by night or got up o' mornin's worried over the question o' how I was goin' to get the swag to pay my rent. Compared to this'—with a wave of his hand at the raging of the elements along Broadway—'Reading gaol was heaven, sir; and since I was discharged I've been a helpless, hopeless wanderer, sleepin' in doorways, chilled to the bone, half-starved, with not a friendly eye in sight, and nothin' to do all day long and all night long but move on when the Bobbies tell me to, and think about the happiness I'd left behind me when I left Reading. Was you ever homesick, governor?'

"I confessed to an occasional feeling of nostalgia for old Picadilly and the Thames.

"'Then you know,' says he, 'how I feels now in a strange land, dreamin' of my comfortable little cell at Reading; the good meals, the pleasant keepers, and a steady job with nothin' to worry about for ten short years. I want to go back, governor—I want to go back!'

"Well," said Holmes, lighting a cigar, "I was pretty nearly floored, but when the door of the saloon blew open and a blast of sharp air and a flurry of snow came in, I couldn't blame the poor beggar—certainly any place in the world, even a jail, was more comfortable than Broadway at that moment. I explained to him, however, that as far as Reading gaol was concerned, I was powerless to help him.

"'But there's just as good prisons here, ain't there, governor?' he pleaded.

"'Oh yes,' said I, laughing at the absurdity of the situation. 'Sing Sing is a first-class, up-to-date penitentiary, with all modern improvements, and a pretty select clientele.'

"'Couldn't you put me in there, governor?' he asked, wistfully. 'I'll do anything you ask, short o' murder, governor, if you only will.'

"'Why don't you get yourself arrested as a vagrant?' I asked. 'That'll give you three months on Blackwell's Island and will tide you over the winter.'

"''Tain't permanent, governor,' he objected. 'At the end o' three months I'd be out and have to begin all over again. What I want is something I can count on for ten or twenty years. Besides, I has some pride, governor, and for Nervy Jim to do three months' time—Lor', sir, I couldn't bring myself to nothin' so small!'

"There was no resisting the poor

cuss, Jenkins, and I promised to do what I could for him."

"That's a nice job," said I. "What can you do?"

"That's what stumps me," said Raffles Holmes, scratching his head in perplexity. "I've set him up in a small tenement down on East Houston Street temporarily, and meanwhile, it's up to me to land him in Sing Sing, where he can live comfortably for a decade or so, and I'm hanged if I know how to do it. He used to be a first-class second-story man, and in his day was an A-1 snatcher, as his name signifies and my father's diaries attest, but I'm afraid his hand is out for a nice job such as I would care to have anything to do with myself."

"Better let him slide, Raffles," said I. "He introduces the third party element into our arrangement, and that's mighty dangerous."

"True—but consider the literary

value of a chap that's homesick for
jail," he answered, persuasively. "I
don't know, but I think he's new."

Ah, the insidious appeal of that
man! He knew the crack in my
armor, and with neatness and de-
spatch he pierced it, and I fell.

"Well—" I demurred.

"Good," said he. "We'll consider
it arranged. I'll fix him out in a
week."

Holmes left me at this point, and
for two days I heard nothing from
him. On the morning of the third
day he telephoned me to meet him
at the stage-door of the Metropolitan
Opera-House at four o'clock. "Bring
your voice with you," said he, enigmatically, "we may need it." An
immediate explanation of his meaning was impossible, for hardly were
the words out of his mouth when he
hung up the receiver and cut the connection.

"I wanted to excite your curiosity

so that you would be sure to come,"
he laughed, when I asked his meaning
later. "You and I are going to join
Mr. Conried's selected chorus of edu-
cated persons who want to earn their
grand opera instead of paying five
dollars a performance for it."

And so we did, although I objected
a little at first.

"I can't sing," said I.

"Of course you can't," said he.
"If you could you wouldn't go into
the chorus. But don't bother about
that, I have a slight pull here and
we can get in all right as long as we
are moderately intelligent, and able-
bodied enough to carry a spear. By-
the-way, in musical circles my name
is Dickson. Don't forget that."

That Holmes had a pull was shortly
proven, for although neither of us
was more than ordinarily gifted
vocally, we proved acceptable and
in a short time found ourselves
enrolled among the supernumeraries

who make of "Lohengrin" a splendid
spectacle to the eye. I found real
zest in life carrying that spear, and
entered into the spirit of what I
presumed to be a mere frolic with
enthusiasm, merely for the experience of it, to say nothing of the
delight I took in the superb music,
which I have always loved.

And then the eventful night came.
It was Monday and the house was
packed. On both sides of the curtain everything was brilliant. The
cast was one of the best and the
audience all that the New York
audience is noted for in wealth,
beauty, and social prestige, and,
in the matter of jewels, of lavish
display. Conspicuous in respect to
the last was the ever-popular, though
somewhat eccentric Mrs. Robinson-
Jones, who in her grand-tier box
fairly scintillated with those marvellous gems which gave her, as a
musical critic, whose notes on the

opera were chiefly confined to observations on its social aspects, put it,
"the appearance of being lit up by
electricity." Even from where I
stood, as a part and parcel of the
mock king's court on the stage, I
could see the rubies and sapphires
and diamonds loom large upon the
horizon as the red, white, and blue
emblem of our national greatness to
the truly patriotic soul. Little did I
dream, as I stood in the rear line of
the court, clad in all the gorgeous
regalia of a vocal supernumerary,
and swelling the noisy welcome to
the advancing Lohengrin, with my
apology for a voice, how intimately
associated with these lustrous head-
lights I was soon to be, and as
Raffles Holmes and I poured out our
souls in song not even his illustrious
father would have guessed that he
was there upon any other business
than that of Mr. Conried. As far as
I could see, Raffles was wrapt in the

music of the moment, and not once, to my knowledge, did he seem to be aware that there was such a thing as an audience, much less one individual member of it, on the other side of the footlights. Like a member of the Old Choral Guard, he went through the work in hand as nonchalantly as though it were his regular business in life. It was during the intermission between the first and second acts that I began to suspect that there was something in the wind beside music, for Holmes's face became set, and the resemblance to his honorable father, which had of late been so marked, seemed to dissolve itself into an unpleasant suggestion of his other forbear, the acquisitive Raffles. My own enthusiasm for our operatic experience, which I took no pains to conceal, found no response from him, and from the fall of the curtain on the first act it seemed to me as if he were trying to avoid me. So marked indeed did this desire to hold himself aloof become that I resolved to humor him in it, and instead of clinging to his side as had been my wont, I let him go his own way, and, at the beginning of the second act, he disappeared. I did not see him again until the long passage between Ortrud and Telramund was on, when, in the semi-darkness of the stage, I caught sight of him hovering in the vicinity of the electric switch-board by which the lights of the house are controlled. Suddenly I saw him reach out his hand quickly, and a moment later every box-light went out, leaving the auditorium in darkness, relieved only by the lighting of the stage. Almost immediately there came a succession of shrieks from the grand-tier in the immediate vicinity of the Robinson-Jones box, and I knew that something was afoot. Only a slight commotion in the

audience was manifest to us upon
the stage, but there was a hurrying
and scurrying of ushers and others
of greater or less authority, until
finally the box - lights flashed out
again in all their silk-tasselled illumi-
nation. The progress of the opera
was not interrupted for a moment,
but in that brief interval of black-
ness at the rear of the house some one
had had time to force his way into
the Robinson-Jones box and snatch
from the neck of its fair occupant that
wondrous hundred - thousand - dollar
necklace of matchless rubies that had
won the admiring regard of many
beholders, and the envious interest
of not a few.

Three hours later Raffles Holmes
and I returned from the days and
dress of Lohengrin's time to affairs
of to-day, and when we were seated
in my apartment along about two
o'clock in the morning, Holmes lit
a cigar, poured himself out a liberal

dose of Glengarry, and with a quiet smile, leaned back in his chair.

"Well," he said, "what about it?"

"You have the floor, Raffles," I answered. "Was that your work?"

"One end of it," said he. "It went off like clock-work. Poor old Nervy has won his board and lodging for twenty years all right."

"But—he's got away with it," I put in.

"As far as East Houston Street," Holmes observed, quietly. "To-morrow I shall take up the case, track Nervy to his lair, secure Mrs. Robinson-Jones's necklace, return it to the lady, and within three weeks the Snatcher will take up his abode on the banks of the Hudson, the only banks the ordinary cracksman is anxious to avoid."

"But how the dickens did you manage to put a crook like that on the grand-tier floor?" I demanded.

"Jenkins, what a child you are!"

laughed Holmes. "How did I get
him there? Why, I set him up with
a box of his own, directly above the
Robinson-Jones box—you can always
get one for a single performance if
you are willing to pay for it—and
with a fair expanse of shirt-front, a
claw-hammer and a crush hat almost
any man who has any style to him
at all these days can pass for a gentleman. All he had to do was to go to
the opera-house, present his ticket,
walk in and await the signal. I gave
the man his music cue, and two
minutes before the lights went out
he sauntered down the broad stair-
case to the door of the Robinson-
Jones box, and was ready to turn
the trick. He was under cover of
darkness long enough to get away
with the necklace, and when the
lights came back, if you had known
enough to look out into the auditorium you would have seen him
back there in his box above, taking

in the situation as calmly as though he had himself had nothing whatever to do with it."

"And how shall you trace him?" I demanded. "Isn't that going to be a little dangerous?"

"Not if he followed out my instructions," said Holmes. "If he dropped a letter addressed to himself in his own hand-writing at his East Houston Street lair, in the little anteroom of the box, as I told him to do, we'll have all the clews we need to run him to earth."

"But suppose the police find it?" I asked.

"They won't," laughed Holmes. "They'll spend their time looking for some impecunious member of the smart set who might have done the job. They always try to find the sensational clew first, and by day after to-morrow morning four or five poor but honest members of the four-hundred will find when they read the morning papers that they are under surveillance, while I, knowing exactly what has happened will have all the start I need. I have already offered my services, and by ten o'clock tomorrow morning they will be accepted, as will also those of half a hundred other detectives, professional and amateur. At eleven I will visit the opera-house, where I expect to find the incriminating letter on the floor, or if the cleaning women have already done their work, which is very doubtful, I will find it later among the sweepings of waste paper in the cellar of the opera-house. Accompanied by two plain-clothes men from headquarters I will then proceed to Nervy's quarters, and, if he is really sincere in his desire to go to jail for a protracted period, we shall find him there giving an imitation of a gloat over his booty."

"And suppose the incriminating letter is not there?" I asked. "He may have changed his mind."

"I have arranged for that," said Holmes, with a quick, steely glance at me. "I've got a duplicate letter in my pocket now. If he didn't drop it, I will."

But Nervy Jim was honest at least in his desire for a permanent residence in an up-to-date penitentiary, for, even as the deed itself had been accomplished with a precision that was almost automatic, so did the work yet to be done go off with the nicety of a well-regulated schedule. Everything came about as Holmes had predicted, even to the action of the police in endeavoring to fasten the crime upon an inoffensive and somewhat impecunious social dangler, whose only ambition in life was to lead a cotillion well, and whose sole idea of how to get money under false pretences was to make some over-rich old maid believe that he loved her for herself alone and in his heart scorned her wealth. Even he

profited by this, since he later sued
the editor who printed his picture
with the label "A Social Highwayman" for libel, claiming damages of
$50,000, and then settled the case
out of court for $15,000, spot cash.
The letter was found on the floor
of the box where Nervy Jim had
dropped it; Holmes and his plain-
clothes men paid an early visit at
the East Houston Street lodging-
house, and found the happy Snatcher
snoring away in his cot with a smile
on his face that seemed to indicate
that he was dreaming he was back
in a nice comfortable jail once more;
and, as if to make assurance doubly
sure, the missing necklace hung about
his swarthy neck! Short work was
made of the arrest; Nervy Jim,
almost embarrassingly grateful, was
railroaded to Sing Sing in ten days'
time, for fifteen years, and Raffles
Holmes had the present pleasure and
personal satisfaction of restoring the

lost necklace to the fair hands of Mrs. Robinson-Jones herself.

"Look at that, Jenkins!" he said, gleefully, when the thing was all over. "A check for $10,000."

"Well—that isn't so much, considering the value of the necklace," said I.

"That's the funny part of it," laughed Holmes. "Every stone in it was paste, but Mrs. Robinson-Jones never let on for a minute. She paid her little ten thousand rather than have it known."

"Great Heavens!—really?" I said.

"Yes," said Holmes, replacing the check in his pocket-book. "She's almost as nervy as Nervy Jim himself. She's what I call a dead-game sport."

IX

THE ADVENTURE OF ROOM 407

RAFFLES HOLMES and I had walked up‑town together. It was a beastly cold night, and when we reached the Hotel Powhatan my companion suggested that we stop in for a moment to thaw out our frozen cheeks, and, incidentally, warm up the inner man with some one of the spirituous concoctions for which that hostelry is deservedly famous. I naturally acquiesced, and in a moment we sat at one of the small tables in the combination reading‑room and café of the hotel.

"Queer place, this," said Holmes, gazing about him at the motley company of guests. "It is the gathering place of the noted and the notorious. That handsome six-footer, who has just left the room, is the Reverend Dr. Harkaway, possibly the most eloquent preacher they have in Boston. At the table over in the corner, talking to that golden - haired lady with a roasted pheasant on her head in place of a hat, is Jack McBride, the light-weight champion of the North-west, and—by thunder, Jenkins, look at that!"

A heavy-browed, sharp-eyed Englishman appeared in the doorway, stood a moment, glanced about him eagerly, and, with a gesture of impatience, turned away and disappeared in the throngs of the corridor without.

"There's something doing to bring 'Lord Baskingford' here," muttered Holmes.

"Lord Baskingford?" said I. "Who's he?"

"He's the most expert diamond lifter in London," answered Holmes.

Adventure of Room 407

"His appearance on Piccadilly was a signal always to Scotland Yard to wake up, and to the jewellers of Bond Street to lock up. My old daddy used to say that Baskingford could scent a Kohinoor quicker than a hound a fox. I wonder what his game is."

"Is he a real lord?" I asked.

"Real?" laughed Holmes. "Yes —he's a real Lord of the Lifters, if that's what you mean, but if you mean does he belong to the peerage, no. His real name is Bob Hollister. He has served two terms in Pentonville, escaped once from a Russian prison, and is still in the ring. He's never idle, and if he comes to the Powhatan you can gamble your last dollar on it that he has a good, big stake somewhere in the neighborhood. We must look over the list of arrivals."

We finished our drink and settled the score. Holmes sauntered, in leisurely fashion, out into the office, and, leaning easily over the counter, inspected the register.

"Got any real live dukes in the house to-night, Mr. Sommers?" he asked of the clerk.

"Not to-night, Mr. Holmes," laughed the clerk. "We're rather shy on the nobility to-night. The nearest we come to anything worth while in that line is a baronet — Sir Henry Darlington of Dorsetshire, England. We can show you a nice line of Captains of Industry, however."

"Thank you, Sommers," said Holmes, returning the laugh. "I sha'n't trouble you. Fact is, I'm long on Captains of Industry and was just a bit hungry to-night for a dash of the British nobility. Who is Sir Henry Darlington of Dorsetshire, England?"

"You can' search me," said the clerk. "I'm too busy to study genealogy—but there's a man here who

knows who he is, all right, all right—
at least I judge so from his manner."

"Who's that?" asked Holmes.

"Himself," said Sommers, with a
chuckle. "Now's your chance to ask
him—for there he goes into the Palm
Room."

We glanced over in the direction
indicated, and again our eyes fell
upon the muscular form of "Lord
Baskingford."

"Oh!" said Holmes. "Well—he is
a pretty fair specimen, isn't he! Little too large for my special purpose,
though, Sommers," he added, "so
you needn't wrap him up and send
him home."

"All right, Mr. Holmes," grinned
the clerk. "Come in again some time
when we have a few fresh importa-
tions in and maybe we can fix you
out."

With a swift glance at the open
page of the register, Holmes bade the
clerk good-night and we walked away.

"Room 407," he said, as we moved along the corridor. "Room 407—we mustn't forget that. His lordship is evidently expecting some one, and I think I'll fool around for a while and see what's in the wind."

A moment or two later we came face to face with the baronet, and watched him as he passed along the great hall, scanning every face in the place, and on to the steps leading down to the barber-shop, which he descended.

"He's anxious, all right," said Holmes, as we sauntered along. "How would you like to take a bite, Jenkins? I'd like to stay here and see this out."

"Very good," said I. "I find it interesting."

So we proceeded towards the Palm Room and sat down to order our repast. Scarcely were we seated when one of the hotel boys, resplendent in brass buttons, strutted through between the tables, calling aloud in a shrill voice:

"Telegram for four-o-seven. Four hundred and seven, telegram."

"That's the number, Raffles," I whispered, excitedly.

"I know it," he said, quietly. "Give him another chance—"

"Telegram for number four hundred and seven," called the buttons.

"Here, boy," said Holmes, nerving himself up. "Give me that."

"Four hundred and seven, sir?" asked the boy.

"Certainly," said Holmes, coolly. "Hand it over—any charge?"

"No, sir," said the boy, giving Raffles the yellow covered message.

"Thank you," said Holmes, tearing the flap open carelessly as the boy departed.

And just then the fictitious baronet entered the room, and, as Holmes read his telegram, passed by us, still apparently in search of the unattainable, little dreaming how close at hand was the explanation of his troubles. I was on the edge of nervous prostration, but Holmes never turned a hair, and, save for a slight tremor of his hand, no one would have even guessed that there was anything in the wind. Sir Henry Darlington took a seat in the far corner of the room.

"That accounts for his uneasiness," said Holmes, tossing the telegram across the table.

I read: "Slight delay. Will meet you at eight with the goods." The message was signed: "Cato."

"Let's see," said Holmes. "It is now six-forty-five. Here — lend me your fountain-pen, Jenkins."

I produced the desired article and Holmes, in an admirably feigned hand, added to the message the words: "at the Abbey, Lafayette Boulevard. Safer," restored it in amended form to its envelope.

"Call one of the bell-boys, please," he said to the waiter.

A moment later, a second buttons appeared.

"This isn't for me, boy," said Holmes, handing the message back to him. "Better take it to the office."

"Very good, sir," said the lad, and off he went.

A few minutes after this incident, Sir Henry again rose impatiently and left the room, and, at a proper distance to the rear, Holmes followed him. Darlington stopped at the desk, and, observing the telegram in his box, called for it and opened it. His face flushed as he tore it into scraps and made for the elevator, into which he disappeared.

"He's nibbling the bait all right," said Holmes, gleefully. "We'll just wait around here until he starts, and then we'll see what we can do with Cato. This is quite an adventure."

"What do you suppose it's all about?" I asked.

"I don't know any more than you do, Jenkins," said Holmes, "save this, that old Bob Hollister isn't playing penny-ante. When he goes on to a job as elaborately as all this, you can bet your last dollar that the game runs into five figures, and, like a loyal subject of his Gracious Majesty King Edward VII., whom may the Lord save, he reckons not in dollars but in pounds sterling."

"Who can Cato be, I wonder?" I asked.

"We'll know at eight o'clock," said Holmes. "I intend to have him up."

"Up? Up where?" I asked.

"In Darlington's rooms — where else?" demanded Holmes.

"In four hundred and seven?" I gasped.

"Certainly—that's our headquarters, isn't it?" he grinned.

Adventure of Room 407

"Now see here, Raffles," I began.

"Shut up, Jenkins," he answered. "Just hang on to your nerve—"

"But suppose Darlington turns up?"

"My dear boy, the Abbey is six miles from here and he won't, by any living chance, get back before ten o'clock to-night. We shall have a good two hours and a half to do up old Cato without any interference from him," said Holmes. "Suppose he does come—what then? I rather doubt if Sir Henry Darlington, of the Hotel Powhatan, New York, or Dorsetshire, England, would find it altogether pleasant to hear a few reminiscences of Bob Hollister of Pentonville prison, which I have on tap."

"He'll kick up the deuce of a row," I protested.

"Very doubtful, Jenkins," said Raffles. "I sort of believe he'll be as gentle as a lamb when he finds out what I know—but, if he isn't, well, don't I represent law and order?" and Holmes displayed a detective's badge, which he wore for use in emergency cases, pinned to the inner side of his suspenders.

As he spoke, Darlington reappeared, and, leaving his key at the office, went out through the revolving doorway, and jumped into a hansom.

"Where to, sir?" asked the cabman.

"The Abbey," said Darlington.

"They're off!" whispered Holmes, with a laugh. "And now for Mr. Cato."

We walked back through the office, and, as we passed the bench upon which the bell-boys sat, Raffles stopped before the lad who had delivered the telegram to him.

"Here, son," he said, handing him a quarter, "run over to the newsstand and get me a copy of this months *Salmagundi*—I'll be in the smoking-room."

The boy went off on his errand, and in a few minutes returned with a magazine.

"Thanks," said Holmes. "Now get me my key and we'll call it square."

"Four hundred and seven, sir?" said the boy, with a smile of recognition.

"Yep," said Holmes, laconically, as he leaned back in his chair and pretended to read.

"Gad, Holmes, what a nerve!" I muttered.

"We need it in this business," said he.

The buttons returned and delivered the key of Sir Henry Darlington's apartment into the hands of Raffles Holmes.

Ten minutes later we sat in room 407—I in a blue funk from sheer nervousness, Raffles Holmes as imperturbable as the rock of Gibraltar from sheer nerve. It was the usual style of hotel room, with bath, pictures, telephone, what - nots, wardrobes, and centre-table. The last proved to be the main point of interest upon our arrival. It was littered up with papers of one sort and another: letters, bills receipted and otherwise, and a large assortment of railway and steamship folders. "He knows how to get away," was Holmes's comment on the latter. Most of the letters were addressed to Sir Henry Darlington, in care of Bruce, Watkins, Brownleigh & Co., bankers.

"Same old game," laughed Holmes, as he read the superscription. "The most conservative banking-house in New York! It's amazing how such institutions issue letters indiscriminately to any Tom, Dick, or Harry who comes along and planks down his cash. They don't seem to realize that they thereby unconsciously lend the glamour of their own respectability and credit to people who, instead of travelling abroad, should be locked up in the most convenient penitentiary at home. Aha!" Holmes added, as he ran his eye over some of the other documents and came upon a receipted bill. "We're getting close to it, Jenkins. Here's a receipted bill from Bar, LeDuc & Co., of Fifth Avenue, for $15,000 — three rings, one diamond necklace, a ruby stickpin, and a set of pearl shirt-studs."

"Yes," said I, "but what is there suspicious about that? If the things are paid for—"

"Precisely," laughed Holmes. "They're paid for. Sir Henry Darlington has enough working capital to buy all the credit he needs with Messrs. Bar, LeDuc & Co. There isn't a house in this town that, after a cash transaction of that kind, conducted through Bruce, Watkins, Brownleigh & Co., wouldn't send its own soul up on approval to a nice, clean-cut member of the British aristocracy like Sir Henry Darlington. We're on the trail, Jenkins—we're on the trail. Here's a letter from Bar, LeDuc & Co. — let's see what light that sheds on the matter."

Holmes took a letter from an envelope and read, rapidly:

"Sir Henry Darlington — care of Bruce, Watkins and so forth—dear Sir Henry — We are having some difficulty matching the pearls—they are of unusual quality, but we hope to have the necklace ready for delivery as requested on Wednesday afternoon at the office of Messrs. Bruce, Watkins and so forth, between five and six o'clock. Trusting the delay will not—and so forth—and hoping to merit a continuance of your valued favors, we beg to remain, and so forth, and so forth.

"That's it," said Holmes. "It's a necklace that Mr. Cato is bringing up to Sir Henry Darlington—and, once in his possession—it's Sir Henry for some place on one of these folders."

"Why don't they send them directly here?" I inquired.

"It is better for Darlington to emphasize Bruce, Watkins, Brownleigh & Co., and not to bank too much on the Hotel Powhatan, that's why," said Holmes. "What's the good of having bankers like that back of you if you don't underscore their endorsement? Anyhow, we've discovered the job, Jenkins; to-day is Wednesday, and the 'goods' Cato has to deliver and referred to in his telegram is the pearl necklace of unusual quality—hence not less than a $50,-000 stake."

At this point the telephone bell rang.

"Hello," said Holmes, answering immediately, and in a voice entirely unlike his own. "Yes—what? Oh yes. Ask him to come up."

He hung up the receiver, put a

cigar in his mouth, lit it, and turned to me.

"It's Cato — just called. Coming up," said he.

"I wish to Heavens I was going down," I ejaculated.

"You're a queer duck, Jenkins," grinned Holmes. "Here you are with a front seat at what promises to be one of the greatest shows on earth, a real live melodrama, and all you can think of is home and mother. Brace up—for here he is."

There was a knock on the door.

"Come in," said Holmes, cheerily.

A tall, cadaverous - looking man opened the door and entered. As his eye fell upon us, he paused on the threshold.

"I beg your pardon," he said. "I —I'm afraid I'm in the wrong—"

"Not at all — come in and sit down," said Holmes, cordially. "That is if you are our friend and partner, Cato—Darlington couldn't wait—"

"Couldn't wait?" said Cato.

"Nope," said Holmes. "He was very much annoyed by the delay, Cato. You see he's on bigger jobs than this puny little affair of Bar, LeDuc's, and your failure to appear on schedule time threw him out. Pearls aren't the only chips in Darlington's game, my boy."

"Well — I couldn't help it," said Cato. "Bar, LeDuc's messenger didn't get down there until five minutes of six."

"Why should that have kept you until eight?" said Holmes.

"I've got a few side jobs of my own," growled Cato.

"That's what Darlington imagined," said Holmes, "and I don't envy you your meeting with him when he comes in. He's a cyclone when he's mad and if you've got a cellar handy I'd advise you to get it ready for occupancy. Where's the stuff?"

R. Holmes & Co.

"In here," said Cato, tapping his chest.

"Well," observed Holmes, quietly, "we'd better make ourselves easy until the Chief returns. You don't mind if I write a letter, do you?"

"Go ahead," said Cato. "Don't mind me."

"Light up," said Holmes, tossing him a cigar, and turning to the table where he busied himself for the next five minutes, apparently writing.

Cato smoked away in silence, and picked up Holmes's copy of the *Salmagundi Magazine* which lay on the bureau, and shortly became absorbed in its contents. As for me, I had to grip both sides of my chair to conceal my nervousness. My legs fairly shook with terror. The silence, broken only by the scratching of Holmes's pen, was becoming unendurable and I think I should have given way and screamed had not Holmes suddenly risen and walked to the telephone, directly back of where Cato was sitting.

"I must ring for stamps," he said. "There don't seem to be any here. Darlington's getting stingy in his old age. Hello," he called, but without removing the receiver from the hook. "Hello—send me up a dollar's worth of two-cent stamps—thank you. Good-bye."

Cato read on, but, in a moment, the magazine dropped from his hand to the floor. Holmes was at his side and the cold muzzle of a revolver pressed uncomfortably against his right temple.

"That bureau cover—quick," Raffles cried, sharply, to me.

"What are you doing?" gasped Cato, his face turning a greenish-yellow with fear.

"Another sound from you and you're a dead one," said Holmes. "You'll see what I'm doing quickly enough. Twist it into a rope, Jim,"

he added, addressing me. I did as I
was bade with the linen cover,
snatching it from the bureau, and a
second later we had Cato gagged.
"Now tie his hands and feet with
those curtain cords," Holmes went
on.

Heavens! how I hated the job, but
there was no drawing back now!
We had gone too far for that.

"There!" said Holmes, as we laid
our victim out on the floor, tied hand
and foot and as powerless to speak
as though he had been born deaf and
dumb. "We'll just rifle your chest,
Cato, and stow you away in the bath-
tub with a sofa-cushion under your
head to make you comfortable, and
bid you farewell—not au revoir, Cato,
but just plain farewell forever."

The words were hardly spoken before the deed was accomplished.
Tearing aside poor Cato's vest and
shirt-front, Raffles placed himself in
possession of the treasure from Bar,

LeDuc & Co., after which we lay Darlington's unhappy confederate at full length in the porcelain - lined tub, placed a sofa-cushion under his head to mitigate his sufferings, locked him in, and started for the elevator.

"Great Heavens, Raffles!" I chattered, as we emerged upon the street. "What will be the end of this? It's awful. When Sir Henry returns—"

"I wish I could be there to see," said he, with a chuckle.

"I guess we'll see, quick enough. I leave town to-morrow," said I.

"Nonsense," said Holmes. "Don't you worry. I put a quietus on Sir Henry Darlington. *He'll* leave town to-night, and we'll never hear from him again — that is, not in this matter."

"But how?" I demanded, far from convinced.

"I wrote him a letter in which I said: 'You will find your treasure in the bath-tub,'" laughed Holmes.

"And *that* will drive him from New York, and close his mouth forever!" I observed, sarcastically. "So very likely!"

"No, Jenkins, not that, but the address, my dear boy, the address. I put that message in an envelope, and left it on his table where he'll surely see it the first thing when he gets back to-night, addressed to 'Bob Hollister,' Diamond Merchant, Cell No. 99, Pentonville Prison."

"Aha!" said I, my doubts clearing.

"Likewise—Ho-ho," said Holmes. "It is a delicate intimation to Sir Henry Darlington that somebody is on to his little game, and he'll evaporate before dawn."

A week later, Holmes brought me a magnificent pearl scarf-pin.

"What's that?" I asked.

"Your share of the swag," he answered. "I returned the pearl necklace to Bar, LeDuc & Co., with a full statement of how it came into my possession. They rewarded me with this ruby ring and that stick-pin."

Holmes held up his right hand, on the fourth finger of which glistened a brilliant blood-red stone worth not less than fifteen hundred dollars.

I breathed a sigh of relief.

"I wondered what you were going to do with the necklace," I said.

"So did I—for three days," said Holmes, "and then, when I realized that I was a single man, I decided to give it up. If I'd had a wife to wear a necklace—well, I'm a little afraid the Raffles side of my nature would have won out."

"I wonder whatever became of Darlington," said I.

"I don't know. Sommers says he left town suddenly that same Wednesday night, without paying his bill," Holmes answered.

"And Cato?"

R. Holmes & Co.

"I didn't inquire, but, from what I know of Bob Hollister, I am rather inclined to believe that Cato left the Powhatan by way of the front window, or possibly out through the plumbing, in some way," laughed Holmes. "Either way would be the most comfortable under the circumstances."

X

THE MAJOR-GENERAL'S PEPPER-POTS

I HAD often wondered during the winter whether or no it would be quite the proper thing for me to take my friend Raffles Holmes into the sacred precincts of my club. By some men—and I am one of them—the club, despite the bad name that clubs in general have as being antagonistic to the home, is looked upon as an institution that should be guarded almost as carefully against the intrusion of improper persons as is one's own habitat, and while I should never have admitted for a moment that Raffles was an undesirable chap to have around, I could not deny that in view of certain characteristics which I knew him to possess, the propriety of taking him into "The Heraclean" was seriously open to question. My doubts were set at rest, however, on that point one day in January last, when I observed seated at one of our luncheon-tables the Reverend Dr. Mulligatawnny, Rector of Saint Mammon-in-the-Fields, a highly esteemed member of the organization, who had with him no less a person than Mr. E. H. Merryman, the railway magnate, whose exploits in Wall Street have done much to give to that golden highway the particular kind of perfume which it now exudes to the nostrils of people of sensitive honor. Surely, if Dr. Mulligatawnny was within his rights in having Mr. Merryman present, I need have no misgivings as to mine in having Raffles Holmes at the same table. The predatory instinct in his nature was as a drop of water in the sea to

that ocean of known acquisitiveness
which has floated Mr. Merryman into
his high place in the world of finance,
and as far as the moral side of the
two men was concerned respectively,
I felt tolerably confident that the
Recording Angel's account - books
would show a larger balance on the
right side to the credit of Raffles
than to that of his more famous
contemporary. Hence it was that I
decided the question in my friend's
favor, and a week or two later had
him in at "The Heraclean" for
luncheon. The dining-room was filled with the usual assortment of interesting men—men who had really done
something in life and who suffered
from none of that selfish modesty
which leads some of us to hide our
light under the bushel of silence.
There was the Honorable Poultry
Tickletoe, the historian, whose articles on the shoddy quality of the
modern Panama hat have created

such a stir throughout the hat trade; Mr. William Darlington Ponkapog, the poet, whose epic on the "Reign of Gold" is one of the longest, and some writers say the thickest, in the English language; James Whistleton Potts, the eminent portraitist, whose limnings of his patients have won him a high place among the caricaturists of the age; Robert Dozyphrase, the expatriated American novelist, now of London, whose latest volume of sketches, entitled *Intricacies*, has been equally the delight of his followers and the despair of students of the occult; and, what is more to the purpose of our story, Major-General Carrington Cox, U. S. A., retired. These gentlemen, with others of equal distinction whom I have not the space to name, were discussing with some degree of simultaneity their own achievements in the various fields of endeavor to which their lives had been devoted. They occupied the

The Pepper-pots

large centre-table which has for many a year been the point of contact for the distinguished minds of which the membership of "The Heraclean" is made up; the tennis-net, as it were, over which the verbal balls of discussion have for so many years volleyed to the delight of countless listeners.

Raffles and I sat apart at one of the smaller tables by the window, where we could hear as much of the conversation at the larger board as we wished—so many members of "The Heraclean" are deaf that to talk loud has become quite *de rigueur* there— and at the same time hold converse with each other in tones best suited to the confidential quality of our communications. We had enjoyed the first two courses of our repast when we became aware that General Carrington Cox had succeeded in getting the floor, and as he proceeded with what he had to say, I observed, in spite of his efforts to conceal the fact, that Raffles Holmes was rather more deeply interested in the story the General was telling than in such chance observations as I was making. Hence I finished the luncheon in silence and even as did Holmes, listened to the General's periods— and they were as usual worth listening to.

"It was in the early eighties," said General Cox. "I was informally attached to the Spanish legation at Madrid. The King of Spain, Alphonso XII., was about to be married to the highly esteemed lady who is now the Queen - Mother of that very interesting youth, Alphonso XIII. In anticipation of the event the city was in a fever of gayety and excitement that always attends upon a royal function of that nature. Madrid was crowded with visitors of all sorts, some of them not as desirable as they might be, and here and there, in the neces-

sary laxity of the hour, one or two
perhaps that were most inimical to
the personal safety and general wel-
fare of the King. Alphonso,. like
many another royal personage, was
given to the old Haroun Al Raschid
habit of travelling about at night in
a more or less impenetrable incognito,
much to the distaste of his ministers
and to the apprehension of the police,
who did not view with any too much
satisfaction the possibility of disaster
to the royal person and the conse-
quent blame that would rest upon
their shoulders should anything of a
serious nature befall. To all of this,
however, the King was oblivious, and
it so happened one night that in the
course of his wanderings he met with
the long dreaded mix-up. He and
his two companions fell in with a
party of cut-throats who promptly
proceeded to hold them up. The
companions were speedily put out of
business by the attacking party, and

the King found himself in the midst
of a very serious misadventure, the
least issue from which bade fair to
be a thorough beating, if not an
attempt upon his life. It was at the
moment when his chances of escape
were not one in a million, when, on
my way home from the Legation,
where I had been detained to a very
late hour, I came upon him struggling
in the hands of four as nasty ruffians
as you will find this side of the gal-
lows. One of them held him by the
arms, another was giving him a fairly expert imitation of how it feels to
be garroted, while the other two were
rifling his pockets. This was too
much for me. I was in pretty fit
physical condition at that time and
felt myself to be quite the equal in
a good old Anglo-Saxon fist fight of
any dozen ordinary Castilians, so I
plunged into the fray, heart and soul,
not for an instant dreaming, however,
what was the quality of the person to

whose assistance I had come. My
first step was to bowl over the gar-
roter. Expecting no interference in
his nefarious pursuit and unwarned
by his companions, who were too
busily engaged in their adventure of
loot to observe my approach, he was
easy prey, and the good, hard whack
that I gave him just under his right
ear sent him flying, an unconscious
mass of villanous clay, into the gut-
ter. The surprise of the onslaught
was such that the other three jumped backward, thereby releasing the
King's arms so that we were now two
to three, which in a moment became
two to two, for I lost no time in
knocking out my second man with as
pretty a solar plexus as you ever saw.
There is nothing in the world more
demoralizing than a good, solid blow
straight from the shoulder to chaps
whose idea of fighting is to sneak up
behind you and choke you to death, or
to stick a knife into the small of your

back, and had I been far less expert with my fists, I should still have had an incalculable moral advantage over such riffraff. Once the odds in the matter of numbers were even, the King and I had no further difficulty in handling the others. His Majesty's quarry got away by the simple act of taking to his heels, and mine, turning to do likewise, received a salute from my right toe which, if I am any judge, must have driven the upper end of his spine up through the top of his head. Left alone, his Majesty held out his hand and thanked me profusely for my timely aid, and asked my name. We thereupon bade each other good-night, and I went on to my lodging, little dreaming of the service I had rendered to the nation.

"The following day I was astonished to receive at the Legation a communication bearing the royal seal, commanding me to appear at the palace at once. The summons was obeyed, and, upon entering the palace, I was immediately ushered into the presence of the King. He received me most graciously, dismissing, however, all his attendants.

"'Colonel Cox,' he said, after the first formal greetings were over, 'you rendered me a great service last night.'

"'I, your Majesty?' said I. 'In what way?'

"'By putting those ruffians to flight,' said he.

"'Ah!' said I. 'Then the gentleman attacked was one of your Majesty's friends?'

"'I would have it so appear,' said the King. 'For a great many reasons I should prefer that it were not known that it was I—'

"'You, your Majesty?' I cried, really astonished. 'I had no idea—'

"'You are discretion itself, Colonel Cox,' laughed the King, 'and to assure you of my appreciation of the fact, I beg that you will accept a small gift which you will some day shortly receive anonymously. It will not be at all commensurate to the service you have rendered me, nor to the discretion which you have already so kindly observed regarding the principals involved in last night's affair, but in the spirit of friendly interest and appreciation back of it, it will be of a value inestimable.'

"I began to try to tell his Majesty that my government did not permit me to accept gifts of any kind from persons royal or otherwise, but it was not possible to do so, and twenty minutes later my audience was over and I returned to the Legation with the uncomfortable sense of having placed myself in a position where I must either violate the King's confidence to acquire the permission of Congress to accept his gift, or break the laws by which all who are connected with the diplomatic service, directly or indirectly, are strictly governed. I assure you it was not in the least degree in the hope of personal profit that I chose the latter course. Ten days later a pair of massive golden pepper-pots came to me, and, as the King had intimated would be the case, there was nothing about them to show whence they had come. Taken altogether, they were the most exquisitely wrought speci-mens of the goldsmith's artistry that I had ever seen, and upon their under side was inscribed in a cipher which no one unfamiliar with the affair of that midnight fracas would even have observed—'A. R. to C. C.'—Alphonso Rex to Carrington Cox being, of course, the significance thereof. They were put away with my other belong-ings, and two years later, when my activities were transferred to London, I took them away with me.

"In London I chose to live in chambers, and was soon established

at No. 7 Park Place, St. James's, a
more than comfortable and centrally
located apartment - house where I
found pretty much everything in the
way of convenience that a man situ-
ated as I was could reasonably ask for.
I had not been there more than six
months, however, when something
happened that made the ease of
apartment life seem somewhat less
desirable. That is, my rooms were
broken open during my absence over
night on a little canoeing trip to
Henley, and about everything valuable in my possession was removed,
including the truly regal pepper-pots
sent me by his Majesty the King of
Spain, that I had carelessly left standing upon my sideboard.

"Until last week," the General continued, "nor hide nor hair of any of
my stolen possessions was ever discovered, but last Thursday night I
accepted the invitation of a gentleman well known in this country as a

leader of finance, a veritable Captain
of Industry, the soul of honor and
one of the most genial hosts imagi-
nable. I sat down at his table at eight
o'clock, and, will you believe me, gentlemen, one of the first objects to
greet my eye upon the brilliantly set
napery was nothing less than one of
my lost pepper-pots. There was no
mistaking it. Unique in pattern, it
was certain of identification anyhow,
but what made it the more certain
was the cipher 'A. R. to C. C.'"

"And of course you claimed it?"
asked Dozyphrase.

"Of course I did nothing of the
sort," retorted the General. "I trust
I am not so lacking in manners. I
merely remarked its beauty and
quaintness and massiveness and general artistry. My host expressed
pleasure at my appreciation of its
qualities and volunteered the information that it was a little thing he
had picked up in a curio shop on

Regent Street, London, last summer. He had acquired it in perfect good faith. What its history had been from the time I lost it until then, I am not aware, but there it was, and under circumstances of such a character that although it was indubitably my property, a strong sense of the proprieties prevented me from regaining its possession."

"Who was your host, General?" asked Tickletoe.

The General laughed. "That's telling," said he. "I don't care to go into any further details, because some of you well-meaning friends of mine might suggest to Mr.—ahem—ha— well, never mind his name—that he should return the pepper-pot, and I know that that is what he would do if he were familiar with the facts that I have just narrated."

It was at about this point that the gathering broke up, and, after our cigars, Holmes and I left the club.

The Pepper-pots

"Come up to my rooms a moment," said Raffles, as we emerged upon the street. "I want to show you something."

"All right," said I. "I've nothing in particular to do this afternoon. That was a rather interesting tale of the General's, wasn't it?" I added.

"Very," said Holmes. "I guess it's not an uncommon experience, however, in these days, for the well-to-do and well-meaning to be in possession of stolen property. The fact of its turning up again under the General's very nose, so many years later, however, that is unusual. The case will appear even more so before the day is over if I am right in one of my conjectures."

What Raffles Holmes's conjecture was was soon to be made clear. In a few minutes we had reached his apartment, and there unlocking a huge iron-bound chest in his bed-room, he produced from its capacious depths another gold pepper-pot. This he handed to me.

"There's the mate!" he observed, quietly.

"By Jove, Raffles—it must be!" I cried, for beyond all question, in the woof of the design on the base of the pepper-pot was the cipher "A. R. to C. C." "Where the dickens did you get it?"

"That was a wedding - present to my mother," he explained. "That's why I have never sold it, not even when I've been on the edge of starvation."

"From whom—do you happen to know?" I inquired.

"Yes," he replied. "I do know. It was a wedding - present to the daughter of Raffles by her father, my grandfather, Raffles himself."

"Great Heavens!" I cried. "Then it was Raffles who—well, you know. That London flat job?"

"Precisely," said Raffles Holmes.

The Pepper-pots

"We've caught the old gentleman red-handed."

"Well, I'll be jiggered!" said I. "Doesn't it beat creation how small the world is."

"It does indeed. I wonder who the chap is who has the other," Raffles observed.

"Pretty square of the old General to keep quiet about it," said I.

"Yes," said Holmes. "That's why I'm going to restore this one. I wish I could give 'em both back. I don't think my old grandfather would have taken the stuff if he'd known what a dead-game sport the old General was, and I sort of feel myself under an obligation to make amends."

"You can send him the one you've got through the express companies, anonymously," said I.

"No," said Holmes. "The General left them on his sideboard, and on his sideboard he must find them.

R. Holmes & Co.

If we could only find out the name of his host last Thursday—"

"I tell you—look in the *Sunday Gazoo* supplement," said I. "They frequently publish short paragraphs of the social doings of the week. You might get a clew there."

"Good idea," said Holmes. "I happen to have it here, too. There was an article in it last Sunday, giving a diagram of Howard Vandergould's new house at Nippon's Point, Long Island, which I meant to cut out for future reference."

Holmes secured the *Gazoo*, and between us, we made a pretty thorough search of its contents, especially "The Doings of Society" columns, and at last we found it, as follows:

"A small dinner of thirty was given on Thursday evening last in honor of Mr. and Mrs. Wilbur Rattington, of Boston, by Mrs. Rattington's brother, John D. Bruce, of Bruce, Watkins & Co., at the latter's residence, 74— Fifth Avenue.

The Pepper-pots

Among Mr. Bruce's guests were Mr. and Mrs. W. K. Danderveldt, Mr. and Mrs. Elisha Scroog, Jr., Major-General Carrington Cox, Mr. and Mrs. Henderson Scovill, and Signor Caruso.''

"Old Bruce, eh?" laughed Holmes. "Sans peur et sans reproche. Well, that is interesting. One of the few honest railroad bankers in the country, a pillar of the church, a leading reformer and—a stolen pepper-pot on his table! Gee!"

"What are you going to do now?" I asked. "Write to Bruce and tell him the facts?"

Holmes's answer was a glance.

"Oh cream-cakes!" he ejaculated, with profane emphasis.

A week after the incidents just described he walked into my room with a small package under his arm.

"There's the pair!" he observed, unwrapping the parcel and displaying its contents—two superb, golden pep-

per-pots, both inscribed "A. R. to
C. C." "Beauties, aren't they?"

"They are, indeed. Did Bruce
give it up willingly?" I asked.

"He never said a word," laughed
Holmes. "Fact is, he snored all the
time I was there."

"Snored?" said I.

"Yes—you see, it was at 3.30 this
morning," said Holmes, "and I went
in the back way. Climbed up to the
extension roof, in through Bruce's
bedroom window, down-stairs to the
dining-room, while Bruce slept unconscious of my arrival. The house
next to his is vacant, you know, and
it was easy travelling."

"You—you—" I began.

"Yes—that's it," said he. "Just
a plain, vulgar bit of second - story
business, and I got it. There were a
lot of other good things lying around,"
he added, with a gulp, "but—well, I
was righting a wrong this time, so
I let 'em alone, and, barring this, I

The Pepper-pots

didn't deprive old Bruce of a bloom-
ing thing, not even a wink of sleep."

"And now what?" I demanded.

"It's me for Cedarhurst — that's
where the General lives," said he.
"I'll get there about 11.30 to-night,
and as soon as all is quiet, Jenkins,
your old pal, Raffles Holmes, will
climb easily up to the piazza, gently
slide back the bolts of the French
windows in the General's dining-
room, proceed cautiously to the sideboard, and replace thereon these two
souvenirs of a brave act by a good
old sport, whence they never would
have been taken had my grandfather
known his man."

"You are taking a terrible risk,
Raffles," said I, "you can just as
easily send the things to the General
by express, anonymously."

"Jenkins," he replied, "that suggestion does you little credit and
appeals neither to the Raffles nor to
the Holmes in me. Pusillanimity was

a word which neither of my forebears could ever learn to use. It was too long, for one thing, and besides that it was never needed in their business."

And with that he left me.

"Well, General," said I to General Cox, a week later at the club, "heard anything further about your pepper-pots yet?"

"Most singular thing, Jenkins," said he. "The d——d things turned up again one morning last week, and where the devil they came from, I can't imagine. One of them, how-ever, had a piece of paper in it on which was written 'Returned with thanks for their use and apologies for having kept them so long.'"

The General opened his wallet and handed me a slip which he took from it.

"There it is. What in thunder do you make out of it?" he asked.

It was in Raffles Holmes's hand-writing.

The Pepper-pots

"Looks to me as though Bruce also had been robbed," I laughed.

"Bruce? Who the devil said anything about Bruce?" demanded the General.

"Why, didn't you tell us he had one of 'em on his table?" said I, reddening.

"Did I?" frowned the General. "Well, if I did, I must be a confounded ass. I thought I took particular pains not to mention Bruce's name in the matter."

And then he laughed.

"I shall have to be careful when Bruce comes to dine with me not to have those pepper-pots in evidence," he said. "He might ask embarrassing questions."

And thus it was that Raffles Holmes atoned for at least one of the offences of his illustrious grandsire.

THE END

THE PROMISE